Edward G. Dyson

Rhymes from the Mines, and other Lines

Edward G. Dyson

Rhymes from the Mines, and other Lines

ISBN/EAN: 9783337271428

Printed in Europe, USA, Canada, Australia, Japan

Cover: Foto ©Andreas Hilbeck / pixelio.de

More available books at **www.hansebooks.com**

RHYMES

FROM THE MINES

AND

OTHER LINES

RHYMES FROM THE MINES
And Other Lines

By EDWARD DYSON

Author of "A Golden Shanty."

Sydney

ANGUS AND ROBERTSON

89 CASTLEREAGH STREET.

1896

Sydney: Geo. Murray & Co., Ltd., Printers.

PREFACE.

The greater part of the material contained in this volume has appeared in the pages of *The Bulletin*, Sydney, from time to time during the last eight years. 'The Rescue' and 'Peter Simson's Farm' were published originally in the Melbourne *Argus*. I have to thank the proprietors of both journals for their courtesy in permitting me to reproduce the verses.

Several pieces, including 'Waiting for Water,' 'The Prospectors,' 'The Tale of Steven,' and 'The Deserted Homestead,' are now printed for the first time.

EDWARD DYSON.

TO THE MEN OF THE MINES

We specked as boys o'er worked-out ground
   By littered flat and muddy stream,
We watched the whim horse trudging round,
   And rode upon the circling beam,
Within the old uproarious mill
   Fed mad, insatiable stamps,
Mined peaceful gorge and gusty hill
With pan, and pick, and gad, and drill,
   And knew the stir of sudden camps.

By yellow dams in summer days
   We puddled at the tom; for weeks
Went seeking up the tortuous ways
   Of gullies deep and hidden creeks.
We worked the shallow leads in style,
   And hunted fortune down the drives,
And missed her, mostly by a mile—
Once by a yard or so. The while
   We lived untrammelled, easy lives.

7

Through blazing days upon the brace
*   We laboured, and when night had passed*
Beheld the glory and the grace
*   Of wondrous dawns in bushlands vast.*
We heard the burdened timbers groan
*   In deep mines murmurous as the seas*
On long, lone shores by drear winds blown.
We've seen heroic deeds, and known
*   The digger's joys and tragedies.*

I write in rhyme of all these things,
*   With little skill, perhaps, but you,*
To whom each tale a memory brings
*   Of bygone days, will know them true.*
Should mates who've worked in stope and face,
*   Who've trenched the hill and swirled the dish,*
Or toiled upon the plat and brace,
Find pleasure in the lines I trace,
*   No better welcome could I wish.*

CONTENTS

CONTENTS

RHYMES

FROM THE MINES

AND

OTHER LINES

THE OLD WHIM HORSE

He's an old grey horse, with his head bowed sadly,
   And with dim old eyes and a queer roll aft,
With the off-fore sprung and the hind screwed badly
   And he bears all over the brands of graft;
And he lifts his head from the grass to wonder
   Why by night and day now the whim is still,
Why the silence is, and the stampers' thunder
   Sounds forth no more from the shattered mill.

In that whim he worked when the night winds
      bellowed
   On the riven summit of Giant's Hand,
And by day when prodigal Spring had yellowed
   All the wide, long sweep of enchanted land;
And he knew his shift, and the whistle's warning,
   And he knew the calls of the boys below;
Through the years, unbidden, at night or morning,
   He had taken his stand by the old whim bow.

But the whim stands still, and the wheeling swallow
  In the silent shaft hangs her home of clay,
And the lizards flirt and the swift snakes follow
  O'er the grass-grown brace in the summer day ;
And the corn springs high in the cracks and corners
  Of the forge, and down where the timber lies ;
And the crows are perched like a band of mourners
  On the broken hut on the Hermit's Rise.

All the hands have gone, for the rich reef paid out,
  And the company waits till the calls come in ;
But the old grey horse, like the claim, is played out,
  And no market's near for his bones and skin.
So they let him live, and they left him grazing
  By the creek, and oft in the evening dim
I have seen him stand on the rises, gazing
  At the ruined brace and the rotting whim.

The floods rush high in the gully under,
  And the lightnings lash at the shrinking trees,
Or the cattle down from the ranges blunder
  As the fires drive by on the summer breeze.
Still the feeble horse at the right hour wanders
  To the lonely ring, though the whistle's dumb,
And with hanging head by the bow he ponders
  Where the whim boy's gone—why the shifts don't
    come.

But there comes a night when he sees lights glowing
  In the roofless huts and the ravaged mill,
When he hears again all the stampers going—
  Though the huts are dark and the stampers still :
When he sees the steam to the black roof clinging
  As its shadows roll on the silver sands,
And he knows the voice of his driver singing,
    And the knocker's clang where the braceman
      stands.

See the old horse take, like a creature dreaming,
  On the ring once more his accustomed place ;
But the moonbeams full on the ruins streaming
  Show the scattered timbers and grass-grown brace.
Yet *he* hears the sled in the smithy falling,
  And the empty truck as it rattles back,
And the boy who stands by the anvil, calling ;
    And he turns and backs, and he ' takes up slack.'

While the old drum creaks, and the shadows shiver
  As the wind sweeps by, and the hut doors close,
And the bats dip down in the shaft or quiver
  In the ghostly light, round the grey horse goes ;
And he feels the strain on his untouched shoulder,
  Hears again the voice that was dear to him,
Sees the form he knew—and his heart grows bolder
  As he works his shift by the broken whim.

He hears in the sluices the water rushing
  As the buckets drain and the doors fall back :
When the early dawn in the east is blushing,
  He is limping still round the old, old track.
Now he pricks his ears, with a neigh replying
  To a call unspoken, with eyes aglow,
And he sways and sinks in the circle, dying ;
  From the ring no more will the grey horse go.

In a gully green, where a dam lies gleaming,
  And the bush creeps back on a worked-out claim,
And the sleepy crows in the sun sit dreaming
  On the timbers grey and a charred hut frame,
Where the legs slant down, and the hare is squatting
  In the high rank grass by the dried-up course,
Nigh a shattered drum and a king-post rotting
  Are the bleaching bones of the old grey horse.

CLEANING UP

When the horse has been unharnessed and we've
    flushed the old machine,
And the water o'er the sluice is running evenly and
    clean ;
When there's thirty load before us, and the sun is
    high and bright,
And we've worked from early morning and shall have
    to work till night,
Not a man of us is weary, though the graft is pretty
    rough,
If we see the proper colour showing freely through
    the stuff.

With a dandy head of water and a youngster at the
    rear
To hand along the billy, boys, and keep the tail race
    clear,
We lift the wash and flash the fork and make the
    gravel fly.

The shovelling is heavy and we're soaked from heel
    to thigh ;
But it makes a fellow tireless and his thews and
    sinews tough
If the colour's showing freely as he gaily shifts the
    stuff.

When Geordie Best is pumping to a rollicking
    refrain,
And Sandy wipes his streaming brow and shakes the
    fork again,
The pebbles dance and rattle and the water seems
    to laugh—
Good luck is half the battle and good will's the
    other half ;
And no day's too long and trying and no toil is hard
    enough,
When we see the colour showing in each shovelful
    of stuff.

Can the mining speculator with a pile of golden
.   scrip,
Or the plunger who has laid his all upon a winning
    tip,
Or the city man who's hit upon a profitable deal,
Know the wonderful elation that the lucky diggers
    feel

When Fortune's smiled but grimly and the store-
man's looking gruff,
And at last they see the colour showing freely in the
stuff ?

Never, mates ! It is a feeling that no other winner
knows—
Not the soldier marching homeward from the conquest of his foes,
Nor the scholar who's successful in his searching of
the skies,
Nor the squalid miser grovelling where his secret
treasure lies.
'Tis a keener, wilder rapture in the digger bold and
bluff
Who feeds the sluice and sees the colour shining in
the stuff.

Then lift the wash, and flash the fork, and make the
gravel fly !
We can laugh at all the pleasures on which other
men rely,
When the water o'er the sluice is running evenly
and clean,
And the loaded ripples glitter with a lively golden
sheen.
No day's too long and trying, and no toil is hard
enough,
When we wash her down and see the colour freely
through the stuff.

There's a sudden, fierce clang of the knocker, then
    the sound of a voice in the shaft,
Shrieking words that drum hard on the centres, and
    the braceman goes suddenly daft:
'Set the whistle a-blowing like blazes! Billy, run,
    give old Mackie a call—
Run, you fool! Number Two's gone to pieces, and
    Fred Baker is caught in the fall!
Say, hello! there below—any hope, boys, any chances
    of saving his life?
'Heave away!' says the knocker. They've started,
    God be praised, he's no youngsters or wife!'

Screams the whistle in fearful entreaty, and the wild
    echo raves on the spur,
And the night, that was still as a sleeper in soft,
    charméd sleep, is astir
With the fluttering of wings in the wattles, and the
    vague, frightened murmur of birds,

With far cooeys that carry the warning, running
    feet, inarticulate words.
From the black belt of bush come the miners, and
    they gather by Mack on the brace,
Out of breath, barely clad, and half-wakened, with a
    question in every face.

'Who's below?' 'Where's the fall?' 'Didn't I
    tell you?—Didn't I say that them sets wasn't
    sound?'
'Is it Fred? He was reckless was Baker; now
    he's seen his last shift underground.'
'And his mate? Where is Sandy M'Fadyn?'
    'Sandy's snoring at home on his bunk.'
'Not at work! Name o' God! a foreboding?' 'A
    foreboding be hanged! He is drunk!'
'Take it steady there, lads!' the boss orders. He
    is white to the roots of his hair.
'We may get him alive before daybreak if he's close
    to the face and has air.'

In the dim drive with ardour heroic two facemen
    are pegging away.
Long and Coots in the rise heard her thunder, and
    they fled without word or delay
Down the drive, and they rushed for the ladders, and
    they went up the shaft with a run,

For they knew the weak spot in the workings, and
    they guessed there was graft to be done.
Number Two was pitch dark, and they scrambled to
    the plat and they made for the face,
But the roof had come down fifty yards in, and the
    reef was all over the place.

Fresher men from the surface replace them, and
    they're hauled up on top for a blow;
When a life and death job is in doing there's room
    only for workers below.
Bare-armed, and bare-chested, and brawny, with a
    grim, meaning set of the jaw,
The relay hurries in to the rescue, caring not for
    the danger a straw ;
'Tis not toil, but a battle, they're called to, and like
    Trojans the miners respond,
For a dead man lies crushed 'neath the timbers, or a
    live man is choking beyond.

By the faint, yellow glow of the candles, where the
    dank drive is hot with their breath,
On the verge of the Land of the Shadow, waging
    war breast to bosom with Death,
How they struggle, these giants ! and slowly, as the
    trucks rattle into the gloom,

Inch by inch they advance to the conquest of a
    prison—or is it a tomb?
And the workings re-echo a volley as the timbers
    are driven in place;
Then a whisper is borne to the toilers: ' Boys, his
    mother is there on the brace!'

Like veterans late into action, fierce with longing
    to hew and to hack,
Riordan's shift rushes in to relieve them, and the
    toil-stricken men stagger back.
' Stow the stuff, mates, wherever there's stowage!
    Run the man on the brace till he drops!
There's no time to think on this billet! Bark the
    heels of the trucker who stops!
Keep the props well in front, and be careful. He's
    in there, and alive, never fret.'
But the grey dawn is softening the ridges, and the
    word has not come to us yet.

Still the knocker rings out, and the engine shrieks
    and strains like a creature in pain
As the cage rushes up to the surface and drops back
    into darkness again.
By the capstan a woman is crouching. In her eyes
    neither hope nor despair;

But a yearning that glowers like frenzy bids those
    who'd speak pity forbear.
Like a figure in stone she is seated till the labour of
    rescue be done.
For the father was killed in the Phœnix, and the son
    —Lord of pity! the son?

'Hello! there on top!' they are calling. 'They are
    through! He is seen in the drive!'
'They have got him—thank Heaven! they've got
    him, and oh, blesséd be God, he's alive!'
'Man on! heave away!' 'Step aside, lads; let his
    mother be first when he lands.'
She was silent and strong in her anguish; now she
    babbles and weeps where she stands,
And the stern men, grown gentle, support her at the
    mouth of the shaft, till at last
With a rush the cage springs to the landing, and her
    son's arms encircle her fast.

She has cursed the old mine for its murders, for the
    victims its drives have ensared,
Now she cries a great blessing upon it for the one
    precious life it has spared.

From her home beyond the river in the parting of
    the hills,
  Where the wattles fleecy blossom surged and
    scattered in the breeze,
And the tender creepers twined about the chimneys
    and the sills,
  And the garden flamed with colour like an Eden
    through the trees,

She would come along the gully, where the ferns
    grew golden fair,
  In the stillness of the morning, like the spirit of
    the place,
With the sunshafts caught and woven in the meshes
    of her hair,
  And the pink and white of heathbloom sweetly
    blended in her face.

She was fair, and small, and slender-limbed, and
 buoyant as a bird,
 Fresh as wild, white, dew-dipped violets where
  the bluegum's shadow goes,
And no music like her laughter in the joyous bush
 was heard,
 And the glory of her smile was as a sunbeam in a
  rose.

Ben felt mighty at the windlass when she watched
 him hauling stuff,
 And she asked him many questions, 'What was
  that?' and 'Why was this?'
Though his bashfulness was painful, and he answered
 like a muff,
 With his foolish 'My word, Missie!' and his
  'Beg your pardon, Miss.'

He stood six foot in his bluchers, stout of heart and
 strong of limb;
 For her sake he would have tackled any man or
  any brute;
Of her half a score of suitors none could hold a
 light to him,
 And he owned the richest hole along the Bullock
  Lead to boot.

Yet while Charley Mack and Hogan, and the Teddy-
    waddy Skite
  Put in many pleasant evenings at 'The Bower,'
    Ben declined,
And remained a mere outsider, and would spend one
    half the night
  Waiting, hid among the trees, to watch her shadow
    on the blind.

He was laughed at on the river, and as far as
    Kiley's Still
  They would tell of Bashful Gleeson, who was
    ' gone on' Kitty Dwyer,
But, beyond defeating Hogan in a pleasant Sunday
    mill,
  Gleeson's courtship went no further till the
    morning of the fire.

We were called up in the darkness, heard a few
    excited words ;
  In the garden down the flat a Chow was thumping
    on a gong ;
There were shouts and cooeys on the hills, and
    cries of startled birds,
  But we saw the gum leaves redden, and that told
    us what was wrong.

O'er 'The Bower' the red cloud lifted as we
    sprinted for the punt.
  Gleeson took the river for it in the scanty clothes
    he wore.
Dwyer was madly calling Kitty when we joined the
    men in front;
  Whilst they questioned, hoped, and wondered, Ben
    was smashing at the door.

He went in amongst the smoke, and found her room ;
    but some have said
  That he dared not pass the threshold—that he
    lingered in distress,
Game to face the fire, but not to pluck sweet Kitty
    from her bed—
  And he knocked and asked her timidly to 'please
    get up and dress.'

Once again he called, and waited till a keen flame
    licked his face ;
  Then a Spartan-like devotion welled within the
    simple man,
And he shut his eyes and ventured to invade the
    sacred place,
  Found the downy couch of Kitty, clutched an
    armful up, and ran.

True or not, we watched and waited, and our hearts
    grew cold and sick
  Ere he came; we barely caught him as the flame
    leapt in his hair.
He had saved the sheets, a bolster, and the blankets,
    and the tick ;
  But we looked in vain for Kitty—pretty Kitty
    wasn't there !

And no wonder : whilst we drenched him as he lay
    upon the ground,
  And her mother wailed entreaties that it wrung
    our hearts to hear,
Hill came panting with the tidings that Miss Kitty
    had been found,
  Clad in white, and quite unconscious, 'mid the
    saplings at the rear.

   .   .   .   .

We're not certain how it happened, but I've heard
    the women say
  That 'twas Kitty's work.   She saw him when the
    doctor left, they vow,
Swathed in bandages and helpless, and she kissed
    him where he lay.
  Anyhow, they're three years married, and he isn't
    bashful now.

THE WORKED-OUT MINE

On summer nights when moonbeams flow
   And glisten o'er the high, white tips,
And winds make lamentation low,
   As through the ribs of shattered ships,
And steal about the broken brace
   Where pendent timbers swing and moan,
And flitting bats give aimless chase,
   Who dares to seek the mine alone?

The shrinking bush with sable rims
   A skeleton forlorn and bowed,
With pipe-clay white about its limbs
   And at its feet a tattered shroud;
And ghostly figures lurk and groan,
   Shrill whispers sound from ghostly lips,
And ghostly footsteps start the stone
   That clatters sharply down the tips.

36

The engine-house is dark and still,
  The life that raged within has fled ;
Like open graves the boilers chill
  That once with glowing fires were red ;
Above the shaft in measured space
  A rotted rope swings to and fro,
Whilst o'er the plat and on the brace
  The silent shadows come and go.

And there below, in chambers dread
  Where darkness like a fungus clings,
Are lingering still the old mine's dead—
  Bend o'er and hear their whisperings !
Up from the blackness sobs and sighs
  Are flung with moans and muttered fears,
A low lament that never dies,
  And ceaseless sound of falling tears.

My ears intent have heard *their* grief—
  The fitful tones of Carter's tongue,
The strong man crushed beneath the reef,
  The groans of Panton, Praer and Young;
And 'Trucker Bill' of Number Five,
  Along the ruined workings roll ;
For deep in every shoot and drive
  This mine secretes a shackled soul.

Ah! woeful mine, where wives have wept,
  And mothers prayed in anxious pain,
And long, distracting vigil kept,
  You yawn for victims now in vain!
Still to that god, whose shrine you were,
  Is homage done in wild device;
Men hate you as the sepulchre
  That stores their bloody sacrifice.

Skirting the swamp and the tangled scrub,
   Tramping and turning amidst the trees,
Carrying nothing but blankets and grub,
   Careless of pleasure and health and care,
Hither and thither with never a goal,
   Heavy, and solemn, and stiff, and slow,
Seeking a track and a long-lost line,
' Blazed avay to dot lead of mine,'—
   Restless and rickety German Joe.

Down in the gully and up the range,
   Stung by the gale and the hate-hot sun,
Never a greeting to give in change,
   Never a tip from the nearest run,—
Seeking a guide to a golden hole,
   Lost in the lone land long ago,
Left in the keep of the hills and trees;
Jealous to have and to hold are these,
   Hope you may get it, though, German Joe.

'Likely old yarn for a horse marine!
   Struck it, you say, at the river head—
Back where the bellowing bunyip's seen,
   Out beyond everywhere—rich and red;
Left it for tucker, and lost the track,
   Blazed till your arm couldn't strike a blow;
Gravel that gleams with the golden stuff,
Nuggets 'shust like as der plums in duff,'—
   What *are* you giving us, German Joe?'

'Blaze?   Yes; you strike for the Granite Stair,
   Make to the left when you cross the creek,
South till you meet with a monkey bear,
   Tramp in his tracks for about a week;
Then you can travel the sky-line back.
   So long, old chap, if you're bound to go.
Don't you forget when you're rich and great
Who laid you on to the lost lead, mate,—
   Mad as a hatter is German Joe.'

Laugh as they may, they will stand his friends,
   Right as rain when the old man takes
Down to his bunk in the hut, and spends
   Seven weeks fighting the fever and shakes,
Muttering still of his lucky lead:
   'Vhisper—I leds you all in der kuow,
Den you pe richer nor as der pank.'
Boys, he's a man if he is a crank—
   Whisky and physic for German Joe.

Now he's abroad in a wild dream-land,
  Baring his breast to the river breeze —
Out where the rock-ribbed ridges stand,
  Telling his tale to the secret trees,
Swift as the shadows his visions glide
  Over the plains where the mad winds blow.
Cover his face now, and carve a stone,
Henceforth his spirit must seek alone—
  Dead as a door-nail is German Joe.

Bushmen have yarned of a ghost that went
  Blazing a track from the Granite Stair
Down to a shaft and a tattered tent,
  Many days' journey from anywhere.
Others have said that the bushmen lied.
  Liars or not, it is true, we know,
Men have discovered a golden mine
Out in the track of an old blazed line,
  Led by the spirit of German Joe.

WAITING FOR WATER

'Twas old Flynn, the identity, told us
   That the creek always ran pretty high,
But that fossicking veteran sold us,
   And he lied as his quality lie.
Through a tangle of ranges and ridges,
   Down a track that is blazed with our hide,
Over creeks minus crossings and bridges,
High and low, mere impertinent midges
   Trying falls with the mighty Divide,

We came, hauling the boxes and stampers,
   Or just nipping them in with a winch;
Now and then in unfortunate scampers
   Missing smash by the eighth of an inch;
Round the spurs very daintily crawling,
   With one team pulling out in a row,
And another lot heavenward hauling,
Lest the whole bag-of-tricks should go sprawling
   Into regions unheard of below,

42

We came through with the shanks and the shafting,
  And the frames, and the wonderful wheel;
Then we put in a month of hard grafting
  Ere we nailed down the last scrap of deal.
She beat true, and with scarce a vibration,
  And we voted her queen of the mills,
And a push from the wide desolation
Drifted in to our jollification
  When her drumming was heard in the hills.

Now the discs by the cam-shaft are rusting,
  And the stamps in the boxes are still,
And a silence that's deep and disgusting
  Seems to hang like a pall on the mill.
Just a fortnight she ran—then she rested,
  And we've little to do but complain;
For a bird in the feed-pipe has nested,
And we've spent every stiver invested,
  And are praying for tucker and rain.

Billy's Creek—theme of eloquent fables—
  Drips like sweat on the breast of the wheel,
And the blankets are dry on the tables,
  And the sluice-box is warped like an eel;
Sudden dust-clouds run lunatic races
  In the red, rocky bed down below,
And the porcupine scrambles in places
Where Flynn swears by the faith he embraces,
  Fourteen inches of water should flow.

For a time we were proof against sorrow,
　　And we harboured a cheerful belief
In the plenteous rains of to-morrow
　　As we belted away at the reef.
We piled quartz in the paddocks and hopper,
　　And the pack-horse came in once a week :
Now our credit is not worth a copper
At the township, and highly improper
　　Is the language the storekeepers speak.

We no longer talk brightly, or snivel
　　Of our luck, but we loaf very hard, .
Too disgusted to care to be civil,
　　And too lazy to look at a card.
Only George finds some slight consolation
　　Crushing prospects—a couple a day—
And then proving by multiplication
How much metal is in the formation,
　　And the 'divvies' she'll probably pay.

But our leisure is qualified slightly
　　By the cattle from over the Fly—
Who have taken to pegging out nightly
　　In our limited water supply.
And the snakes have assisted in keeping
　　Things alive, for the man, you'll agree,
Will be spry who may find he's been sleeping
With a tiger—or chance on one creeping
　　In the water he wanted for tea.

Though our sweltering sky never changes,
   Squatter Clark, up at Crowfoot, complains
That prospectors out over the ranges
   Have been chased out of camp by the rains.
Veal, the Methodist preacher at Spence's,
   Who the Cousin Jacks say is 'some tuss'
As a rain-making parson, commences
To enlarge on *our* sins and offences,
   And to blame all his failures on us.

We don't go to his church down the mountain :
   Seven miles is a wearisome trot,
With the glass playing up like a fountain,
   And the prayers correspondingly hot.
So on Sunday each suffering sinner
   Has a simple, convivial spree,—
A roast porcupine, maybe, for dinner ;
For we daily grow thinner and thinner
   On the week's bread and treacle and tea.

We've been scared, too, of late by Golightly,
   Him who kept up his chin best of all,
And predicted with confidence nightly
   Heavy rains that neglected to fall,
And enlarged on the sure indications
   (While we listened, and wearily groaned)
Of tremendous climatic sensations,
Fearful tempests, and great inundations,
   That, it happened, were always postponed.

He's gone daft through our many reverses,
   Or the sun has got on to his brain,
For he cowers all day, and he curses
   To a fretful and wearing refrain;
And at midnight he dolefully screeches
   In the gloom of the desolate mill;
Or he goes in his shirt, making speeches
To the man in the moon, whom he reaches
   From the summit of Poverty Hill.

So we're waiting, and watching, and longing
   With an impotent, bitter desire,
And new troubles and old ones come thronging,
   Drought, and fever, and famine, and fire;
And we know—our misfortunes reviewing—
   All the pangs that in Hades betide,
Where the damned sit eternally stewing,
And, through days never ending, are suing
   For the water that's ever denied.

'Twas a sleepy little chapel by a wattled hill erected,
  Where the storms were always muffled, and an
    atmosphere of peace
Hung about beneath the gum-trees, and the garden
    was respected
  By the goats from Billybunga and the washer-
    woman's geese.
In the week-days it was sacred to my young
    imagination;
  From its walls there oozed a sentiment of reverence
    profound;
And on Sabbath morns the murmuring of the childish
    congregation
  Seemed to spread a benediction in the bush land
    far around.

47

But when Brother Peetree prayed all the parrots
 flew dismayed,
And the hill shook to its centre, and the trees and
 fences swayed;
And we youngsters heard the rumble of the Day of
 Judgment there,
When the pious superintendent wrestled manfully
 in prayer.

They were horny-handed Methodists, and men of
 scanty knowledge,
  Who controlled that 'little corner of the vine-
  yard' by the pound;
Their theology was not the kind that's warranted
 at college,
  But their faith was most abundant, and their
  gospel always sound.
Brother Peetree was a miner at the Band of Hope.
 His leisure
  He employed in 'sticking porkers' for his
  neighbours, and his skill
Was a theme of admiration; but his soul's sublimest
 pleasure
  Was to speak a prayer on Sunday in the chapel
  'neath the hill.

Froze the marrow in our bones at the sound of
    hollow groans,
And the shrieks of moral anguish, and the awful
    thunder tones ;
And we saw the Hell-fire burning, and we smelt it
    in the air,
When dear Brother Peetree struggled with the Lord
    of Hosts in prayer.

Brother Peetree always started with a murmured
    supplication,
Knelt beside a form, serenely, with a meek,
    submissive face ;
But he rose by certain stages to a rolling ex-
    hortation,
And a wild, ecstatic bellowing for sanctity and
    grace ;
And he threw his arms to heaven, and the seats went
    down before him
As he fought his way along the aisle, and prayed
    with might and main,
With hysterical beseechings. Then a sudden peace
    fell o'er him,
And he finished, sobbing softly, at his starting-
    point again.

And the elders, to their ears pale with reverential
 fears,

And the sisters and the choir indulged in hot,
 repentant tears ;

And the sinners for salvation did with eagerness
 declare,

When beloved Brother Peetree wrestled mightily in
 prayer.

THE OLD CAMP-OVEN

We don't keep a grand piano in our hut beside the
    creek,
And I'm pretty certain Hannah couldn't bang it,
    anyhow,
But we've got one box of music, and I'd rather hear
    its squeak
Than the daisiest cantata that's been fashioned up
    to now.
It's an old camp-oven merely, with a handle made of
    wire,
But no organ built could nearly compensate to me
    for it
When I come off graft and find it playing tunes
    before the fire,
And I'm feeling sort of vacant, but just wonder-
    fully fit.

In its sizzle, sizzle, sizzle,
There's a thousand little airs,
And no man can sit and grizzle
'Bout his troubles and his cores
While the flames are gaily winding,
And the tea is down to brew,
And the old camp-oven's grinding
All the reels he ever knew.

When the wet winds meet and whip me in the early
winter nights,
And the hissing hailstones clip me all the way across
the flat,
As I battle for'ards, water-logged, toward the
beckoning lights,
There is always there a welcome to console a chap
for that.
For my little wife is beaming brisk and bright beside
the lamp,
And the old camp-oven's going. Gosh! I feel just
like a kid
As I peel and sluice so slippy, and I hear the storm
winds vamp
To the singing of the oven when the missus lifts
the lid.

There's a sizzle and a splutter
  And a whirr of many harps;
Where's the instrument can utter
  Such a maze of flats and sharps ?
Not for me the great creations
  When the old camp-oven plays
' *Home Sweet Home,' with variations,*
  At the end of working days.

In the evenings dim and hazy, stretched outside
    along a butt,
Feeling reasonably lazy, blowing clouds that curl
    and climb,
I can hear the old camp-oven on the logs before the
    hut
Ripping out a mellow chorus that just suits the place
    and time.
If we strike it in the ranges, or The Windmill turns
    out well,
I suppose there'll be some changes, and I'll want to
    make things gee ;
But the time will never happen when I'll be so
    steep a swell
That the old camp-oven's measure won't be melody
    to me.

'Neath its bubble, bubble, bubble,
  There's the lilt of jigs and reels ;
All the common kind of trouble
  That the horney-handed feels
Is wiped out in half a minute
  By the restfulness it brings,
And the peaceful rapture in it
  When the old camp-oven sings.

'That's the boiler at The Bell, mates! Tumble out,
    Ned, neck and crop—
Never mind your hat and coat, man, we'll be wanted
    on the job.
Barney's driving, Harvey's stoking—God help all
    the hands on top!
Bring along the brandy, some one. Don't stand
    like an image, Bob;
Grab those shirts—they'll all be needed. Rugs
    and candles, that's all right.
Bet your lives, boys, we'll have lots of doctor's work
    to do to-night!

'Didn't she thunder? Scot! I thought the
    universe had gone to smash.
Take the track through Peetree's paddock, make
    the smartest time you know.

Barney swore her plates were rotten, but poor Bill
    was always rash.'
'And his missus, heaven help her!—they were
    spliced a month ago.'
Down the track we raced together, up the hill—then
    o'er the claim
Saw the steam-clouds hanging thickly, lustrous with
    the glow of flame.

Boiler-house in hopeless ruins, engines wrecked and
    smoke-stack gone ;
Bricks and shingles widely scattered, and the
    shattered boiler bare.
'Five men missed!' 'Buck in, you fellows; get
    your freest action on ;
Keep the fire back from the timber—God knows
    who is under there.
Sprag that knocker. How it rattles ! Braceman's
    nowhere—Coleman's Joe.
Tell them what has happened, Ryan. They will
    have to wait below.'

As we fought the fires, the women, pale and tearful
    gathered round.
'That you, Peter ? Thanks to Heaven !' 'There's
    my Harry! God is good !'

' Praise the Lord—they've got our lad safe! Joe
 the braceman has been found !'
Down between the tips they found him, pinned
 there by a log of wood.
'Battery boys are safe. Mack saw them hiding
 under Peetree's ricks.
They just up and cut from under when it started
 raining bricks.'

Only two now—Bill and Barney. Still we laboured
 might and main
'Mid the ruins round the boiler where the shattered
 walls were stacked.
Then his wife discovered Barney, dazed and black,
 but right as rain ;
Said he didn't know what hit him—'thought the
 crack of doom had cracked ;'
He had landed on the sand-heap, thirty yards or so
 away.
' God *is* mighty good to sinners,' murmured Geordie.
 'Let us pray.'

Fifty voices called on Harvey, and we worked like
 horses all,
Delving down amongst the timber, burnt and
 knocked about, but gay.

' Lend a hand here, every man ; he's pinned beneath
    the outer wall !

All together.   Now you've got him.   Gently does
    it.   That's O.K.

Scalded !   Yes, and right arm broken.   Pass some
    brandy, one of you.

Cheer, ye devils !   Give it lip, lads.   He's alive and
    kicking, too ! '

' Give him air, now.   Make a track there.   Let him
    see his missus first.'

' Where's his wife ? '   The women wondered.   She
    had not been seen all night.

Someone whispered she was timid, that she dared not
    face the worst.

Harvey smiled despite his troubles.   ' Boys, she's
    fainted—she's all right.'

So we bore him gaily home, and as he saw the
    gateway near

Bill tried hard to lead the chorus when we gave a
    rousing cheer.

' Stop, for God's sake ! '   In the garden, where her
    life blood tinged the vine,

Prone poor Harvey's wife was lying, in the moon-
    light, cold and gray.

There the flying bolt had struck her as she ran
    towards the mine.
We could guess the truth too well—and near a
    broken firebar lay.
Carrol, kneeling down beside her, gently raised the
    wounded head,
And we bent to catch his whisper, and he answered
    sadly—' Dead ! '

THE TRUCKER

If you want a game to tame you and to take your
      measure in,
Try a week or two of trucking in a mine
Where the rails are never level for a half-a-minute's
      spin,
And the curves are short and sharp along the line.

Try the feverish bottom level, down five hundred
      feet of shaft,
Where the atmosphere is like a second suit,
When the wash is full of water, and you've got to
      run the graft,
For there's forty ton of gravel in the shoot.

'Want a job o' truckin', dost tha?' says the boss,
      old Geordie Rist,
'Shift's a trucker short, ma lad, but aw don' know—
Can'st tha do th' work, though, think'st tha? Art
      a pretty decent fist?
Eh, well, damme! thoo can try it; go below.'

So the cage is manned, the knocker clangs and
    clatters on the brace,
The engine draws a deep, defiant breath
To inflate her lungs of iron ; and in silence, face to
    face,
We drop into the darkness deep as death.

Then a fairy sense of lightness and of floating on
    the night,
A sudden glare, and Number Three is passed ;
Soon a sound of warring waters and another rush of
    light—
'All clear !' The up-trip never seems so fast.

It is rough upon the tyro, that first tussle with the
    trucks—
The wretched four with worn, three-cornered
    wheels
That are sure to fall to his lot and to floor him if
    his pluck's
Not true when mates are grinding at his heels.

Then the struggle at the incline, and the deucéd
    ticklish squeeze
At the curves where strength alone not all avails,
And the floundering in the mullock, and the badly-
    broken knees
Before he learns to run upon the rails.

But it's like all other grafting, and the man that
    has the grit
Won't tucker out with one back-racking shift;
When he's sweated to condition, with his muscles
    firm and fit,
He'll disdain to stick at seven trucks of drift.

He can swarm around the pinches with a scramble
    and a dash,
And negotiate the inclines just as pat;
And the sheets of iron rattle and the waters surge
    and splash
As he shoots the ' full 'uns ' in along the plat.

When the empties wind and clatter down the drive
    and through the dark—
As ' blowing ' spells those backward journeys
    serve—
On before, deep set in darkness, glints and glows a
    feeble spark,
The candle burning dimly at the curve.

After cribs are polished off, and when the smoke
    begins to rise
And cling about the caps and in the cracks,
There's a passing satisfaction in the patriarchal
    lies
Of the Geordie pioneers and Cousin Jacks—

Lanky Steve's unwritten stories of the fun of
     Fifty-two,
Or the dashing days at Donkey Woman's Flat,
Of traps, and beaks, and heavy yields, and pugilists
     put through,
And lifting up the flag at Ballarat.   .

Yes, the truckers' toil is rather heavy grafting as a
     rule—
Much heavier than the wages, well I know;
But the life's not full of trouble, and the fellow is
     a fool
Who cannot find some pleasure down below.

'STOP-AND-SEE'

I'm stewing in a brick-built town ;
  My coat is quite a stylish cut,
And, morn and even, up and down,
  I travel in a common rut ;
But as the city sounds recede,
  In dreamy moods I sometimes see
A vision of a busy lead,
  And hear its voices calling me.

My flaccid muscles seem to tweak
  To feel the windlass pull and strain,
To shake the cradle by the creek,
  And puddle at the ' tom' again.
I'd gladly sling this musty shop
  To see the sluicing waters flow—
A pile of tucker, dirt on top,
  And simply Lord knows what below.

'Twas lightly left, 'tis lately mourned,
  The tent life up at Stop-and-See,
When shirts with yellow clay adorned
  Were badges of nobility,
When Sunday's best was Monday's wear,
  And Bennett gave us verse and book—
Poor Dick! a crude philosopher,
  But, bless his heart, a clever cook.

An easy life we lived and free;
  The wash was only ten-weight stuff,
The 'bottom' dry and soft at knee—
  With Hope to help us 'twas enough.
Then none could say us ay or nay
  Did we agree to slave or smoke;
The pan was ready with the pay
  E'en though the graft was half in joke.

'Twas good when 'spell-oh!' had been said,
  To watch the white smoke curl and cling
Against the gravel roof o'erhead,
  The candles dimly flickering
And circled with a yellow glow—
  To sprawl upon the broken reef,
And pensively to pull and blow
  The fragrant incense from the leaf.

And where the creek ran by our tent,
　Or lingered through embowered ponds,
In dusky nooks that held a scent
　Of musk amid the drooping fronds,
It was a pleasant task to lay
　The dish within the stream, and there
To puddle off the pug and clay,
　And pan the gleaming prospect bare.

Oft in the strange deceit of dreams,
　I swirl the old tin-dish again,
And Wondee's rippling water seems
　To cool my weary limbs as then ;
And down the hill-side bare and dry
　A digger's chorus faintly comes,
And mingles with the lullaby
　Of locusts in the drowsy gums.

The barrels rattle on their stands,
　And in the shafts the nail-kegs swing.
The short, sharp strokes of practised hands
　Are making pick and anvil ring.
I hear the splitter's measured blow,
　The distant knocker rise and drop,
The cheery cry, ' Look up, below !'
　The muffled call of ' Heave, on top !'

No piles were made at Stop-and-See,
   No nuggets found of giant size,
But, looking back, it seems to me
   That all who laboured there were wise.
For there was freedom void of pride,
   There hate of forms and shallow arts,
And there were friendships all too wide
   For narrow streets and narrow hearts

IN 'THE BENEVOLENT'

I'm off on the wallaby!' cries Old Ben,
  And his pipe is lit, and his swag is rolled;
There is nothing here for us old-time men,
  But up north, I hear, they are on the gold.'
And he shuffles off with a feeble stride,
  With his ragged swag and his billy black.
He is making tracks for the other side,
O'er the river deep, or the Great Divide;
  But at night, dead beat, he travels back.

Then at morn next day he is off again,
  With an eager light in his aged eyes,
Tramping away on his journey vain
  For the land of promise beyond the rise.
Over the range there is work to do,
  There is roaring life at the shanty bars.
He will tramp the plains whilst the skies are blue,
And will wander the great wide bushland through,
  And be soothed to sleep by the blinking stars.

In the garden gay where the old man roams
 Pied poppies sway on their supple stalks,
And the fair white rose on the soft breeze foams,
 And the pansies peep by the gravelled walks ;
But his brow by the breeze of the hills is fanned,
 And the clink of bells to his quick ear comes.
When he shades his eyes with a withered hand,
He sees silent rivers and ranges grand,
 Or a still lagoon under silver gums.

' Are you bound out back, Dan ? ' the children cry,
 And they peer at him through the fence, and shout
' Well, it's so long, Dan,' as he hobbles by,
 With his ' Ay, ay, sonny lad—tramping out ! '
On his back he's bearing his house and bed,
 As he bore them both in his manhood's pride,
Pressing on each day till his strength has fled
By the force of a dauntless spirit led—
 There's a rush somewhere on the Sydney side.

Though his sight may fail and his limbs give way,
 Yet no weakness touches his brave old heart,
And he cries each night : ' At the break of day
 I must strap up bluey and make a start ! '

And they humour him ; for the time is near
   When he'll tramp no more under changeful skies,
But will leave his travels and troubles here,
Take the track God blazed with His stars, and steer
   To the Never Land just across the rise.

Out of luck, mate? Have a liquor. Hang it
    where's the use complaining?   .
Take your fancy, I'm in funds now—I can stand
    the racket, Dan.
Dump your bluey in the corner; camp here for the
    night, it's raining;
Bet your life I'm glad to see you—glad to see a
    Daylesford man.
Swell? Correct, Dan. Spot the get up; and I own
    this blooming shanty,
Me the fellows christened 'Jonah' at Jim Crow
    and Blanket Flat,
'Cause my luck was so infernal—you remember me
    and Canty?
Rough times, those—the very memory keeps a chap
    from getting fat.

Where'd I strike it? That's a yarn. The fire's a
　　　comfort—sit up nearer.

Hoist your heels, man; take it easy till Kate's ready
　　　with the stew.

Yes, I'll tell my little story; 'taint a long one, but
　　　it's queerer

Than those lies that Tullock pitched us on The Flat
　　　in '52.

Fancy Phil a parson now! He's smug as grease, the
　　　Reverend Tullock.

Yes, he's big—his wife and fam'ly are a high and
　　　mighty lot.

Didn't I say his jaw would keep him when he tired
　　　of punching mullock?

Well, it has—he's made his pile here. How d'you
　　　like your whisky—hot?

Luck! Well, now, I like your cheek, Dan. You
　　　had luck, there's no denying.

I in thirty years had averaged just a wage of
　　　twenty bob—

Why, at Alma there I saw men making fortunes
　　　without trying,

While for days I lived on 'possums, and then had
　　　to take a job.

Bah! *you* talk about misfortune—my ill-luck was
    always thorough :
Gold once ran away before me if I chased it for
    a week.
I was starved at Tarrangower—lived on tick at
    Maryborough—
And I fell and broke my thigh-bone at the start
    of Fiery Creek.

At Avoca Canty left me. Jim, you know, was not
    a croaker,
But he jacked the whole arrangement—found we
    couldn't make a do :
Said he loved me like a brother, but 'twas rough
    upon a joker
When he'd got to fight the devil, and find luck
    enough for two.
Jim was off. I didn't blame him, seeing what he'd
    had to suffer
When Maginnis, just beside us, panned out fifty
    to the tub.
We had pegged out hours before him, and had
    struck another duffer,
And each store upon the lead, my lad, had laid us
    up for grub.

After that I picked up Barlow, but we parted at
　　Dunolly
When we'd struggled through at Alma, Adelaide
　　Lead, and Ararat.
See, my luck was hard upon him; he contracted
　　melancholy,
And he hung himself one morning in the shaft at
　　Parrot Flat.
Ding it? No. Where gold was getting I was on
　　the job, and early,—
Struck some tucker dirt at Armstrong's, and just
　　lived at Pleasant Creek,
Always grafting like a good 'un, never hopeless-like
　　or surly,
Living partly on my earnings, Dan, but largely on
　　my cheek.

Good old days, they like to call them—they were
　　tough old days to many :
I was through them, and they left me still the
　　choice to graft or beg—
Left me gray, and worn, and wrinkled, aged and
　　stumped—without a penny—
With a chronic rheumatism and this darned old
　　twisted leg.

Other work?   That's true—in plenty.   But you
    know the real old stager
Who has followed up the diggings, how he hangs
    on to the pan,
How he hates to leave the pipeclay.   Though you
    mention it I'll wager
That *you* never worked on top until you couldn't
    help it, Dan.

Years went by.   On many fields I worked, and often
    missed a meal, and
Then I found Victoria played out, and the yields
    were very slack,
So I took a turn up Northward, tried Tasmania and
    New Zealand,—
Dan, I worked my passage over, and I sneaked the
    journey back.
Times were worse.   I made a cradle, and went
    fossicking old places ;
But the Chows had been before me, and had
    scraped the country bare ;
There was talk of splendid patches 'mongst the
    creeks and round the races,
But 'twas not my luck to strike them, and I
    think I lived on air.

Rough? That's not the word. So help me, Dan,
    I hadn't got a stiver
When I caved in one fine Sunday—found I
    couldn't lift my head.
They removed me, and the doctor said I'd got
    rheumatic fever,
And for seven months I lingered in a ward upon
    a bed.
Came out crippled, feeling done-up, hopeless-like
    and very lonely,
And dead-beat right down to bed rock as I'd never
    felt before.
Bitter? Just! Those hopeful years of honest graft
    had left me only
This bent leg; and some asylum was the prospect
    I'd in store.

You'll be knowing how I felt then—cleaned-out,
    lame, completely gravelled—
All the friends I'd known were scattered widely
    north, and east, and west:
There seemed nothing there for my sort, and no
    chances if I travelled;
No, my digging days were over, and I had to
    give it best.

Though 'twas hard, I tried to meet it like a man in
    digger fashion :
'Twasn't good enough—I funked it ; I was fairly
    on the shelf,
Cursed my bitter fortune daily, and was always in a
    passion
With the Lord, sir, and with everyone, but mostly
    with myself.

I was older twenty years then than I am this
    blessed minute,
But I got a job one morning, knapping rock at
    Ballarat ;
Two-and-three for two-inch metal. You may say
    there's nothing in it,
To the man who's been through Eaglehawk and
    mined at Blanket Flat.
Wait—you'd better let me finish. Weak and ill, I
    bucked in gladly,
But to get the tools I needed I was forced to
    pawn my swag.
I'd no hope of golden patches, but I needed tucker
    badly,
And this job, I think, just saved me being lum-
    bered on the vag.

Fortune is a fickle party, but in spite of all her
    failings,
Don't revile her, Dan, as I did, while you've still
    a little rope.
Well, the heap that I was put on was some heavy
    quartz and tailings,
That was carted from a local mine, I think the
    Band of Hope.
Take the lesson that is coming to your heart, old
    man, and hug it:
For I started on the heap with scarce a soul to
    call my own,
And in less than twenty minutes I'd raked out a
    bouncing nugget
Scaling close on ninety ounces, and just frosted
    round with stone.

How is that for high, my hearty? Miracle! It
    was, by thunder!
After forty years of following the rushes up and
    down,
Getting old, and past all prospect, and about to
    knuckle under,
Struck it lucky knapping metal in the middle of
    a town!

Pass the bottle! Have another! Soon we'll get
    the word from Kitty—
She's a daisy cook, I tell you. Yes, the public
    business pays ;
But my pile was made beforehand—made it
    ' broking ' in the city.
That's the yarn I pitch the neighbours. Here's to
    good old now-a-days.

NIGHT SHIFT

'Hello! that's the whistle, be moving.
　　Wake up! don't lie muttering there.
What language! your style is improving—
　　It's pleasant to hear you at prayer.
Turn out, man, and spare us the blessing.
　　Crib's cut, and the tea's on the brew.
You'll have to look slippy in dressing
　　For that was the half-hour that blew.'

'Half-past! and the night's simply awful,
　　The hut fairly shakes in the storm.
Hang night-shifts! They shouldn't be lawful;
　　I've only had time to get warm.
I notice the hut's rarely bright, and
　　The bunk's always cold as a stone,
Except when I go on at night, and
　　The half-after whistles have blown.

'Bob built up that fire just to spite me,
    The conscienceless son of a swab!
By Jove! it would fairly delight me
    To let Hogan be hanged with his job.
Oh! it's easy to preach of contentment;
    You're eloquent all on the flute.
Old Nick's everlasting resentment
    Plague Dick if he's taken my boot!

' Great Cæsar! you roasted the liquor,
    Whoever it was made the tea;
It's hotter than hell-broth and thicker!
    Fried bacon again.   Not for me!
Good night, and be hanged!   Stir up, Stumpy,
    You look very happy and warm;
I'll hoist half the bark off the humpy
    And give you a taste of the storm.'

We laughed as he went away growling:
    But down where the wind whipped the creek
The storm like old fury was howling,
    And Fred was on top for the week.
' A devil's own night for the braceman,'
    Muttered Con.   ' It's a comfort to know
All weathers are one to the faceman,
    All shifts are alike down below.'

We slept, and the storm was receding,
  The wind moaned a dirge overhead,
When men brought him, broken and bleeding,
  And laid him again on the bed.
We saw by the flame burning dimly
  The gray hue of death on his face.
The stoker enlightened us grimly :
  'No hope. He was blown from the brace.'

A FRIENDLY GAME OF FOOTBALL

We were challenged by The Dingoes—they'ré the
    pride of Squatter's Gap—
To a friendly game of football on the flat by Devil's
    Trap.
And we went along on horses, sworn to triumph in
    the game,
For the honour of Gyp's Diggings, and the glory of
    the same.

And we took the challenge with us. It was beautiful
    to see,
With its lovely, curly letters, and its pretty filagree.
It was very gently worded, and it made us all feel
    good,
For it breathed the sweetest sentiments of peace
    and brotherhood.

We had Chang, and Trucker Hogan, and the man
    who licked The Plug,
Also Heggarty, and Hoolahan, and Peter Scott, the
    pug ;
And we wore our knuckle-dusters, and we took a
    keg on tap
To our friendly game of football with The Dingoes
    at The Gap.

All the fellows came to meet us, and we spoke like
    brothers dear.
They'd a tip-dray full of tucker, and a waggon load
    of beer,
And some lint done up in bundles ; so we reckoned
    there'd be fun
Ere our friendly game of football with the Dingo
    Club was done.

Their umpire was a homely man, a stranger to the
    push,
With a sweet, deceitful calmness, and a flavour of
    the bush.
He declared he didn't know the game, but promised
    on his oath
To see fair and square between the teams, or paralyse
    them both.

Then we bounced the ball and started, and for twenty
    minutes quite
We observed a proper courtesy and a heavenly
    sense of right,
But Fitzpatrick tipped McDougal in a handy patch
    of mud,
And the hero rose up, chewing dirt, and famishing
    for blood.

Simple Simonsen, the umpire, sorted out the happy
    pair,
And he found a pitch to suit them, and we left
    them fighting there ;
But The Conqueror and Cop-Out met with cries
    of rage and pain,
And wild horses couldn't part those ancient enemies
    again.

So the umpire dragged them from the ruck, and
    pegged them off a patch,
And then gave his best attention to the slugging
    and the match.
You could hardly wish to come across a fairer-
    minded chap
For a friendly game of football than that umpire
    at The Gap.

In a while young Smith, and Henty, and Blue Ben,
    and Dick, and Blake,
Chose their partners from The Dingoes, and went
    pounding for the cake.
Timmy Hogan hit the umpire, and was promptly put
    to bed
'Neath the ammunition waggon, with a bolus on his
    head.

Feeling lonely-like, Magee took on a local star
    named Bent,
And four others started fighting to avoid an
    argument :
So Simonsen postponed the game, for fear some
    slight mishap
Might disturb the pleasant feeling then prevailing
    at The Gap.

Sixty seconds later twenty lively couples held the
    floor,
And the air was full of whiskers, and the grass was
    tinged with gore,
And the umpire kept good order in the interests of
    peace,
Whilst the people, to oblige him, sat severely on the
    p'lice.

Well, we fought the friendly game out, but I
    couldn't say who won ;
We were all stretched out on shutters when the
    glorious day was done ;
Both the constables had vanished ; one was carried
    off to bunk,
And the umpire was exhausted, and the populace
    was drunk.

But we've written out a paper, with good Father
    Feeley's aid,
Breathing brotherly affection ; and the challenge is
    conveyed
To the Dingo Club at Squatter's, and another
    friendly game
Will eventuate at this end, on the flat below
    the claim.

We have pressed The Gap to bring their central
    umpire if they can—
Here we honestly admire him as a fair and decent
    man—
And we're building on a pleasant time beside the
    Phœnix slums,
For The Giant feels he's got a call to plug him if
    he comes.

THE TALE OF STEVEN

'Tis the tale of Simon Steven, braceman at the
    Odd-and-Even,
At The Nations, in the gully. They were sinking
    in the rock.
Sim was small and wiry rather, and a husband and a
    father,
But he's gone and left his family as a consequence
    of shock.

Shock was Sim's disease, we reckoned, for it took
    him in a second,
And no doctor born could dognose what the
    symptoms were, I think.
But we're missin' Sim completely—he could play
    the whistle sweetly,
And was always very sociable and brotherly in
    drink,

That was how poor Steven drifted into trouble—
    being gifted,
He was hungry for an audience, and it led him up
    to Coy's ;
But his wife made no deductions for the artist, and
    the ructions
What she raised around that public were just
    fireworks for the boys.

When she caught him on the liquor, being stronger
    like and quicker,
She would hammer him in company, which, I take
    it, wasn't right ;
Yet he bore it like a martyr while his wife played
    up the tartar,
And she gave her straight opinion of each mother's
    son in sight.

Sim had marks of her corrections scattered round
    in all directions
On his features and his figure, but he didn't seem
    to care—
For he thought his missus clearly did her duty by
    him merely
When she pommelled him for boosing with a poker
    or a chair.

'Twas a Wednesday, boss, I'm thinking. There'd been
    much promiscuous drinking
Up the gully, where some city chaps were
    christening Spooner's mill ;
Sim was dayshift at The Nations, and he missed the
    grand orations,
But, with help from men and brothers, he con-
    trived to get his fill.

They'd been shooting holes, an' Steven, when he
    left the Odd-and-Even,
Carried with him in his pocket here a plug of
    dynamite.
Sim had put it there to soften—which is done by
    miners often,
But it's not the sort of practice that I'd recom-
    mend as right.

Well, the braceman didn't worry after tea that day,
    nor hurry
To the bosom of his family, but took drink for
    drink with Mack ;
When they aimed him homewards kindly, Steven
    went the distance blindly,
And his feet performed the lockstitch all the way
    along the track.

Mrs. Sim was primed and ready, and she met him
    with a neddy,
And she passed no vain remarks, but aimed an
    awful blow at him ;
Came a sound of roaring thunder—Mrs. Sim was
    blown from under,
And the universe was ruined, and the sun went
    out for Sim.

After search in all directions, we found very few
    selections
Of the widow's dear departed, but we did the
    best we could.
For, you see, by passion goaded, and not knowing
    Sim was loaded,
She'd concussed that plug of dynamite, and blown
    him up for good.

There was room for no reproaches 'bout the hearse
    and mourning coaches ;
Though we only buried samples, yet we 'lowed for
    style and tone—
Man's-size coffin, grave, and preacher for a broken
    fellow-creature,
And we wrote ' In Death Divided' at the bottom
    of the stone.

THE FOSSICKER

A straight old fossicker was Lanky Mann,
   Who clung to that in spite of friends' advising :
A grim and grizzled worshipper of ' pan,'
   All other arts and industries despising.

Bare-boned and hard, with thin long hair and beard,
   With horny hands that gripped like iron pliers ;
A clear, quick eye, a heart that nothing feared,
   A soul full simple in its few desires.

No hot, impatient amateur was Jo,
   Sweating to turn the slides up every minute—
He knew beforehand how his stuff would go,
   Could tell by instinct almost what was in it.

I've known him stand for hours, and rock, and rock,
   A-swinging now the shovel, now the ladle,
So sphinx-like that at Time he seemed to mock,
   Resolved to run creation through his cradle.

No sun-shafts pricked him through his seasoned hide,
  Nor cold nor damp could bend his form heroic ;
Bare-breasted Jo the elements defied,
  And met all fortunes like a hoary Stoic.

Where there were tailings, tips, and mangled fields,
  And sluggish, sloven creeks meandering slowly,
Where puddlers old and sluice-sites promised yields,
  There Lanky might be found, contented wholly.

Even though they'd worked the field, as Chinkies do,
  Had 'bulled' each shaft, and scraped out every
      gutter,
Burnt every stick, and put the ashes through—
  Yet Jo contrived to knock out bread and butter,

And something for a dead-broke mate—such men
  As he have little love for filthy lucre ;
His luxury was a whisky now and then,
  And now and then a friendly game of euchre.

They tell me he is dead: 'On top ?   That's so,
  Died at the handle, mate, which is accordin'
As *he* should die and if you're good, you'll know
  Jo pannin' prospects in the River Jordan.'

THE TIN-POT MILL

Quite a proud and happy man is Finn the packer
　　Since he built his crazy mill upon the rise,
And he stands there in the gully, chewing ' backer,'
　　With a sleepy sort of comfort in his eyes,
Gazin' up to where the antiquated jigger
　　Is a-wheezing and a-hopping on the hill,
For up here my lord the Gov'nor isn't bigger
　　Than the owner of the Federation Mill.

　　　　She goes biff, puff, bang, bump, clitter-clatter,
　　　　　　smash,
　　　　And she rattles on for half a shift, and lets up
　　　　　　with a crash ;
　　　　And then silence reigns a little while, and all
　　　　　　the land is still
　　　　While they're tinkering awkward patches on
　　　　　　the tin-pot mill.

94

It's a five-head plant, and mostly built of lumber,
  'Twas erected by a man that didn't know,
And we've never had a decent spell of slumber
  Since that battery of Finn's was got to go;
For she raises just the most infernal clatter,
  And we guessed the Day of Judgment had come
    down
When the tin-pot mill began to bang and batter
  Like an earthquake in a boiler-metal town.

All the heads are different sizes, and the horses
  Are so crazy that the whole caboodle rocks,
And each time a stamper thunders down it forces
  Little spirtings through the crannies in the box.
Then the feed-pipe's mostly plugged and aggravating,
  And the pump it suffers badly from a cough;
Every hour or so they burst a blooming grating,
  And the shoes are nearly always coming off.

Mickey drives her with a portable, a ruin
  That they used for donkeying cargo in the Ark.
When she's got a little way on, and is *doing*,
  You should hear that spavined coffee-grinder bark

She is loose in all her joints, and, through corrosion,
   Half her plates are not a sixteenth in the thick.
We're expecting a sensational explosion,
   And a subsequent excursion after Mick.

From the feed—which chokes—to quite the smallest
     ripple,
   From the bed-logs to the guides, she's mighty
     queer,
And she joggles like an agitated cripple
   With St. Vitus dance intensified by beer.
She stops short; and starts with most unearthly
     rumbles,
   And, distracted by the silence and the din,
Through the sleepless night the weary miner
     grumbles,
   And heaps curses on the family of Finn.

But the owner's much too cute a man to wrangle.
   He is crushing for the public, understand,
And each ton of stuff that's hammered through the
     mangle
   Adds its tribute to the value of his land.
For she leaks the raw amalgam, and he's able
   To see daylight 'twixt the ripples an' the plates,

And below the box and 'neath the shaking-table
There are nest-eggs 'cumulating while he waits.

> She goes biff, puff, bang, bump, clitter-clatter,
> smash,
> And she rattles on for half a shift, and lets up
> with a crash ;
> Then silence reigns a little while, and all
> the land is still
> While they're tinkering awkward patches on
> the tin-pot mill.

A POOR JOKE

' No, you can't count me in, boys; I'm off it—
   I'm jack of them practical jokes;
They give neither pleasure nor profit,
   And the fellers that play them are mokes.
I've got sense, though I once was a duffer,
   And I fooled up my share, I allow,
But since conscience has made me to suffer—
   She's pegging away at me now.

' You notice I've aged rather early,
   And the wrinkles are deep on my face?
That's sorrer—I'm sixty-nine, barely.
   Jes' camp, and I'll tell you my case.
It was here on The Springs, we had hit it,
   And were working the lead on this spot—
And we were, to my shame I admit it,
   A rather unprincipled lot.

' We were drunk all the day on the Sundays—
   No wickeder habit exists ;
And our exercise mostly on Mondays
   Was feats of endurance with fists.
See, the wash wasn't what we'd call wealthy—
   Ten pennyweight stuff, thereabout—
And we took matters easy and healthy ;
   Now we'd rush for the same, I've no doubt.

' Well, one morning, from over the border
   Two Mongols moved inter the camp,
Which we voted a thing out of order—
   The climate for Chows was too damp.
But it happened a couple of troopers
   Arrived on The Springs that same week,
So the Chinks, in their opium stupors,
   Didn't wander down inter the creek,

' Or get drowned in the dam at The Crescent,
   As we reckoned might happen somehow ;
But they settled down, easy and pleasant,
   And there wasn't the smell of a row.
Howsomever, we weren't long twigging
   The Chows were an ignerent pair,
And knew nothin' at all about digging
   And that was our chance to get square.

'It was 'cording to Bastow's directions,
     Though *I* volunteered for the game,
To ensnare their Mongolian affections,
     And lay them right on to a claim
Round the bend where we'd bottomed a duffer—
     Myself and Pat Foley—right there,
Where the sinking is deep and is tougher
     Than the hobs of Gehenna, I swear.

'That shaft was a regular clinker,
     Which it riles me to think of to-day.
Quite a fortnight it took us to sink her,
     And then we came through on the clay,
Not the ghost of a handful of gravel.
     Well, we dropped it without any fuss,
On the hill pegged the best we could snavel,
     And the devil could prospect, for us.

'But the Pagans were not a bit wiser,
     And I counted it pretty fair game
To appear as their friend and adviser,
     And induce them to take up that claim,
By a-cracking the lay and position
     So's to get them to sink on the clay,
Till they struck a hot shop in Perdition
     Or tapped water in Europe some day.

' But the heathens were mighty suspicious,
    Wouldn't have it I cared for their sakes—
Here, I state that all Chinkies are vicious
    And I hate them like fever and snakes.
Then I tried a new system of dealing,
    And offered advice at a fee,
And they caught on like winking.   Fine feeling
    Is wasted on any Chinee.

' So they pegged out our cast-off, the duffer.
    Their rights they had made out exact,
And Ah Kit, who was boss, wouldn't suffer
    Any little neglect of the Act:
And I put in their pegs to a fraction,
    As grave as a brick on a hob,
Rigged up things to their full satisfaction,
    And charged them five quid for the job.

' Well, the heathens soon set their picks going,
    And they seemed rather fond of the graft,
Though the boys had had trouble in stowing
    A heap of dead things in the shaft,
And we chuckled and thought we had got 'em:
    I knew I could tickle the pair
To keep sinking on inter the bottom
    For gravel that never was there.

' Next night a most harrowing rumour
    Went round, and the camp was half daft :
It was said that a nugget—a boomer—
    Had been found by the Chows in our shaft.
'Point of fact, that the Pagans had struck it,
    Had knocked down a sample of wash
That looked good for a pound to the bucket,
    And our joke had gone hopelessly squash.

' It was c'rect, boys, by all that is holy !
    We'd struck a false bottom,* no doubt,
And the fortune of self and of Foley
    Was scooped by Ah Kit and Ah Gout.
We resolved that these Chinese were sapping
    The wealth of the land, and agreed
On a project for catching them napping
    When the troopers rode on to the lead.

---

* It has happened in sinking on alluvial fields that a
streak of the strata (the "bottom") which usually underlies
the wash has been found immediately above it, the result
of a geological freak. This has occasionally deceived even
diggers of some experience, and led them to abandon claims
as duffers which, when subsequently sunk a little further,
have proved to be golden holes.

' Yes, we scrambled for claims all around 'em,
  And we made the foam fly for a week,
But the Chows had the gilt edge. Confound 'em,
  They'd lobbed right on top of the streak !
No, your joke, boys, I reckon is risky,
  And somewhat ridic'lus, I think,
But I'm with you for friendship and whisky
  If one of you orders the drink.'

All was up with Richard Tanner—
  'Wait-a-Bit' we called him.   Dead
Yes.   The braceman dropped a spanner,
  Landed Richard on the head;
Cracked his skull, sir, like a teacup,
  Down the pump-shaft in the well.
Braceman hadn't time to speak up,
  Tanner never knew what fell.

Tell the widow?   Who'd go through it?
  No one on the shift would stir;
But Pat Ryan said he'd do it—
  'Nately break the news to her.'
Pat's a splitter, and a kinder
  Heart I never wish to know.
Stephens told him where to find her,
  Begged him gently deal the blow.

104

In a very solemn manner
   Ryan met the dead man's wife—
' Mornin' to yez, Widdy Tanner!'
   Says he gravely, ' Such is life!'
' I'm no widow!' says she, prying
   For the joke in Ryan's eye.
' 'Scuse me, mum,' says Paddy, sighing,
   ' 'Scuse me, mum, but that's a lie.'

' That remark would be repented
   If Dick Tanner heard,' says she.
' Meanin', mum, the late lamented
   Party av that name?' says he.
Still the widow missed the notion,
   Wonder only filled her eye ;
So Pat smothered his emotion,
   Gulped, and had another try.

' 'Tis like this, ye see, me honey,
   I've been sint t' let ye know ;
Ye've inherited some money—
   Twilve 'r fifteen pounds 'r so.
Through a schame av Providence's,
   Which no mortal man could dodge ;
Poor Dick's funeral expenses
   Have fell due, mum, at the lodge!'

STRUCK IT AT LAST

He was almost blind, and wasted
  With the wear of many years;
He had laboured, and had tasted
  Bitter troubles, many cares;
But his laugh was loud and ringing,
  And his flag was on the mast—
Every day they heard him singing:
  'Bound to strike it rich at last.'

Here he brandished axe and maul ere
  Bnninyong, and after that
Fought and bled with Peter Lalor
  And the boys at Ballarat.
East and west and northward, striving,
  As the tides set fresh and fast—
Ever trying, rarely thriving—
  Yes, he'd strike it rich at last.

Now and then she'd pan out snugly,
   Mostly all the other way,
But he never cut up ugly
   When he bottomed on the clay ;
Never cursed, or got disgusted,
   Mourned the days and chances.past—
Geordie always hoped and trusted
   He would strike it rich at last.

If the days were very dull, or
   When the store-men cut up rough
And he couldn't raise a colour
   From a cart-load of the stuff,
No man found him chicken-hearted,
   He'd no time to bang and blast ;
Pegged her out again and started—
   Bound to strike it rich at last.

Blinded by a shot in Eighty,
   Sinking for the Pegleg Reef,
If he sorrowed o'er his fate, he
   Let no mortal see his grief.
In the Home there in the city
   Geordie won their favor fast,
All the inmates learned his ditty—
   ' Bound to strike it rich at last.'

When brought low, and bowed, and hoary,
  Still his eyes alone were blind,
Fortune left undimmed the glory
  Of his happy, tranquil mind;
In his heart a flame was glowing
  That defied the roughest blast,
And he sang: 'There is no knowing,
  Mates, I'll strike it rich at last.'

As the end approached he prattled
  Of old days at Ballarat,
And again the windlass rattled
  At Jim Crow and Blanket Flat;
And the nurses heard him mutter
  As his dauntless spirit passed:
'Streak of luck, boys! On the gutter!'
  Geordie struck it rich at last.

THE PROSPECTORS

When the white sun scorches the fair, green land in
    the rage of his fierce desires,
Or looms blood red on the Western hills, through
    the smoke of their waning fires ;
When the winds at war strew the mountain side
    with limbs of the mangled trees,
Or the flood tides wheel in the valleys low, or sweep
    to the distant seas,
We are leading back, and the faintest track that we
    leave in the desert wild
Or we blaze for fear through the forest drear will be
    tramped by the settler's child.

We have turned our backs on the City's joys, on the
    glare of its myriad lights,
On the measured peace of its bloodless days, and the
    strife of its shining nights ;

We have fled the pubs in the dull bush towns and
    the furthermost shanty bars,
And have camped away at the edge of space, or aloft
    by the brooding stars.
We have stirred the world as our dishes swirled and
    we drummed on the matted gold,
And from East and West we beguile their best with
    a wonderful tale oft-told.

We go pushing on when the mirage glints o'er the
    rim of the voiceless plain,
And we leave our bones to be finger posts for the
    seekers who come again.
At the jealous heart of the secret bush, we have
    battered with clamour loud
And have made a way for the squatter bold, or a
    path for the busy crowd.
We have gone before through the shadowy door of the
    Never, the Great Unknown,
And have journeyed back with a golden pack, or as
    dust in the wild winds blown.

In the chilling breath of the ice-bound range, we
    have laboured and lost and won ;
On the blazing hills we have striven long in the face
    of the angry sun.

We have fallen spitted with niggers' spears in the
    graves ourselves have dug,
And have bitten grass, with a cloven skull, and the
    turf in our arms to hug.
From our rifled dead have the natives fled, blood-
    drunk, to their camping place,
Whilst the crows enthroned on a limb intoned to the
    devil a measured grace.

We have butchered too when the camp ran wild,
    with a mad, malignant hate,
For the lust of gold, or the hope we had, or the love
    of a murdered mate.
We have shocked the night with our ribald songs in
    the sullen, savage lands,
And have died the death that the lone man dies in
    the grip of the reeling sands,
Or have lived to die in a city sty, with the help of a
    charity prayer,
Or to do the swell at a grand hotel on our thousands
    of pounds a year.

We are moving still, and not love, nor fear, nor a
    wife's nor mother's grief,
Can distract the longing that drives us forth on the
    track of the hidden reef.

Some will face the heathen in lands afar by rivers
    and looming peaks,
Some will stay to ravage their own home hills, or to
    dig by the sluggish creeks,
Some go pushing West on the old, old quest, and
    wherever their tents abide
Will the world flow in and its swift tide spin till it
    scatter them far and wide.

Is it greed alone that impels our ranks? Is it only
    the lust of gold
Drives them past where the sentinel ranges stand,
    where the plains to the sky unfold;
Is there nothing more in this dull unrest that re-
    mains in the hearts of man,
'Till the swag is rolled, or the pack-horse strapped,
    or the ship sails out again?
Is it this alone, or in blood and bone does the ven-
    turous spirit glow
That was noble pride when the world was wide and
    the tracks were all Westward Ho?

We are common men, with the faults of most, and a
    few that ourselves have grown,
With the good traits too of the common herd, and
    some more that are all our own;

We have drunk like beasts, and have fought like
    brutes, and have stolen, and lied, and slain,
And have paid the score in the way of men—in
    remorse and fear and pain.
We have done great deeds in our direst needs in the
    horrors of burning drought,
And at mateship's call have been true through all to
    the death with the Furthest Out.

As the soft breeze stirs all the tender green of the
    bush that is newly born,
And the wattles blaze on the flats and gladden the
    hills with the glow of morn.
We are trenching high in the stony slopes, or
    turning the creeks below,
Or the gorge re-echoes the thud of picks and the
    songs that the miners know.
When the lode strips clean with a yellow sheen our
    fortunes are fairly won ;
When the dish pans bare, up with tents and ware,
    and hurrah ! for the outward run.

OTHER LINES.

PETER SIMSON'S FARM

Simson settled in the timber when his arm was
    strong and true
And his form was straight and limber; and he
    wrought the long day through
In a struggle, single-handed, and the trees fell
    slowly back,
Twenty thousand giants banded 'gainst a solitary Jack.

    Through the fiercest days of summer you
        might hear his keen axe ring
    And re-echo in the ranges, hear his twanging
        crosscut sing;
    Then the great gums swayed and whispered,
        and the birds were skyward blown,
    As the circling hills saluted o'er a bush king
        overthrown.

Clearing, grubbing, in the gloaming, strong in faith
    the man descried
Heifers sleek and horses roaming in his paddocks
    green and wide,
Heard a myriad corn-blades rustle in the breeze's
    soft caress,
And in every thew and muscle felt a joyous
    mightiness.

    So he filled the stubborn forest, hacked and
        hewed with tireless might,
    And a conqueror's peace went with him to his
        fern-strewn bunk at night:
    Forth he strode next morn, delighting in the
        duty to be done,
    Whistling shrilly to the magpies trilling carols
        to the sun.

Back the clustered scrub was driven, and the sun fell
    on the lands,
And the mighty stumps were riven 'tween his bare,
    brown, corded hands.
One time flooded, sometimes parching, still he did
    the work of ten,
And his dog-leg fence went marching up the hills
    and down again.

By the stony creek, whose tiny streams slid
 o'er the sunken bowls
To their secret, silent meetings in the shaded
 water-holes,
Soon a garden flourished bravely, gemmed
 with flowers, and cool and green,
While about the hut a busy little wife was
 always seen.

Came a day at length when, gazing down the paddock
 from his door,
Simson saw his horses grazing where the bush was
 long before,
And he heard the joyous prattle of his children on
 the rocks,
And the lowing of the cattle, and the crowing of the
 cocks.

There was butter for the market, there was
 fruit upon the trees,
There were eggs, potatoes, bacon, and a tidy
 lot of cheese;
Still the struggle was not ended with the
 timber and the scrub,
For the mortgage is the toughest stump the
 settler has to grub.

But the boys grew big and bolder—one, a sturdy,
    brown-faced lad,
With his axe upon his shoulder, loved to go to work
    ' like dad,'
And another in the saddle took a bush-bred native's
    pride,
And he boasted he could straddle any nag his dad
    could ride.

    Though the work went on and prospered there
        was still hard work to do ;
    There were floods, and droughts, and bush
        fires, and a touch of pleuro, too ;
    But they laboured, and the future held no
        prospect to alarm—
    All the settlers said : ' They're stickers up at
        Peter Simson's farm !'

One fine evening Pete was resting in the hush of
    coming night,
When his boys came in from nesting with a
    clamorous delight ;
Each displayed a tiny rabbit, and the farmer eyed
    them o'er,
Then he stamped—it was his habit—and he smote his
    knee and swore.

Two years later Simson's paddocks showed
    dust-coloured, almost bare,
And too lean for hope of profit were the cows
    that pastured there,
And the man looked ten years older. Like
    the tracks about the place
Made by half a million rabbits, were the lines
    on Simson's face.

As he fought the bush when younger, Simson stripped
    and fought again,
Fought the devastating hunger of the plague with
    might and main,
Neither moping nor despairing, hoping still that
    times would mend,
Stubborn browed and sternly facing all the trouble
    Fate could send.

One poor chicken to the acre Simson's land
    will carry now.
Starved, the locusts have departed ; rust is
    thick upon the plough ;
It is vain to think of cattle, or to try to raise
    a crop,
For the farmer has gone under, and the
    rabbits are on top.

So the strong, true man, who wrested from the bush
    a homestead fair,
By the rabbits has been bested ; yet he does not
    know despair—
Though begirt with desolation, though in trouble
    and in debt,
Though his foes pass numeration, Peter Simson's
    fighting yet !

    He is old too soon and failing, but he's game
        to start anew,
    And he tells his hopeless neighbours ' what
        the Gov'mint's *goin'* to do.'
    Both his girls are in the city, seeking places
        with the rest,
    And his boys are tracking fortune in the
        melancholy West.

SINCE NELLIE CAME TO LIVE ALONG THE CREEK

My hut is built of stringy-bark, the window's calico,
The furniture a gin-case, one bush-table, and a
      bunk ;
Thick as wheat on my selection does the towering
      timber grow,
And the stately blue-gums' taproots to the bedrock
      all are sunk ;
  Then the ferns spring up like nettles,
  And the ti-tree comes and settles
On my clearing if I spell-oh for a week ;
  But I work for love of labour
  Since I've got a handy neighbour,
And Miss Nellie's come to live along the creek.

Time was when Death sat by me, and he stalked me
      through the trees ;
Then my arm was weak as water, and my heart a
      weary thing ;

I was sullen as a wombat on such still, wan days as
      these,
And my wedges all were rusty, and my axe had
      lost its ring.
  Then a fear like sickness bound me,
  And I cursed the trees around me,
For quite hopeless seemed the struggle I'd begun ;
  And at night-time, cowed and sinking,
  I would sit there thinking, thinking,
Gazing grimly down the barrels of my gun.

Then I felt the bush must crush me with its dreadful,
      brooding wings,
And its voices seemed to mock me, till I thought
      that I was mad
Like the mopoke, and the jackass, and the other
      loony things ;
For beside my old dog, Brumbie, not a living mate
      I had.
  Then each sapling was a giant,
  And the stumps were all defiant,
And my friends were very few and far to seek ;
  But the bush is bright and splendid,
  And my melancholy's ended,
Since Miss Nellie came to live along the creek !

I would swear she was the sweetest if the world was
     full of girls :
She's as graceful as a sapling, and her waist is neat
     and slim ;
She is dimpled o'er with smiling, and has glossy,
     golden curls,
And her eyes peep out like violets 'neath her sun-
     hat's jealous rim.
  If I think I see her flitting
  On the sun-crowned hill, or sitting
'Neath the fern-fronds where the creek sleeps, deep
     and cool,
  Then my stroke is straight and steady,
  And the white chips run and eddy,
And I laugh aloud at nothing, like a fool.

Now my axe rings like a sabre, and my heart exults
     with pride
When the green gums sweep the scrub down, and
     they thunder and rebound,
And then lie with limbs all shattered, reaching out
     on either side,
Like giants killed in battle, with their faces to the
     ground.
  Now the bush has many pleasures,
  And a wondrous store of treasures,

And a thousand tales its eerie voices speak ;
   But its strange night hushes, seeming
   Sent to lure to mystic dreaming,
Have no terrors, now Miss Nellie's on the creek.

I am happy when the thunder bumps and bellows
     on the hill,
And the tall trees writhe and wrestle with the fury
     of the gale,
Or when sunshine floods the clearing, and the
     bushland is so still
That I hear the creek's low waters tinkle, tinkle on
     the shale.
   In the thought that she is near me
   There's a charm to lift and cheer me,
And a power that makes me mighty seems to flow
   From Miss Nellie's distant coo-ey,
   Or her twin lips red and dewy
When she comes by here, and shyly calls me ' Joe.'

She can work from dawn to nightfall, and look
     handsome all the day ;
At her smile my garden flourished, and the vines
     grew green and strong,
And the bush falls back before it, and it strikes the
     scrub away,

For it lingers ever with me, and it stirs me like a
    song.
  Now I labour in all weathers,
  And the logs are merest feathers,
Nor my heart nor yet my hand is ever weak,
  And a higher thing my prize is
  Than all else that life comprises—
Pretty Nell, who's come to live along the creek.

THE FREAK

Just beyond All Alone, going back,
  Is the humpy of Hatter Magee.
We had travelled all day on the track,
  And he offered us mutton and tea.
Mack is rather reserved, but will speak
  On one theme, and with eloquence too—
That's his angular chestnut, The Freak.
Here's a tale that he told through the week,
  And I try to believe it is true:

' True, he ain't no account ez a nag,
  An' I'm not goin' to boast of his blood ;
If I liked I could pitch you a mag
  'Bout his sire, once a prince of the stud ;
Give performances coloured and plain,
  An' a pedigree long ez my arm—

Which is style, but I'm straight in the main,
So he ain't of the Wangdoodle strain,
   Nor his dam wasn't Kate nor The Charm.

' Fiddle-headed an' spavined! Well, p'raps.
   Yes, his legs is all over the shop,
An' his pacin's described by the chaps
   Ez a sort of a wallaby hop.
He ain't good over sticks, an' a mile
   In four-thirty's his best up to date ;
An' he's jest pure Gehenna fer guile,
But I wouldn't sell out fer a pile,
   'Cause I'm not goin' to dog on a *mate.*

' See, I'm here, and he's yonder, of course,
   But I might 'a' been crow-bait by now—
Once my life seemed to hang on that horse,
   An' I didn't get left. That is how !
They've bin tellin' you—Billy an' Spence ?
   Ah, they're mighty smart men down the creek,
An' they won't allow horses has sense,
But jest guy it ez chance or pretence
   When I tell what was done by The Freak.

' But I'm here, an' he's there—that's enough !
   We were out 'mong the Misery Hills.
'Course you don't know the country. It's rough ;
   An' the man that it corners *it kills.*

I can't figure what happened us quite,
    But we came in a heap, me an' him.
When I knew who I was it was night,
An' my head an' my chest wasn't right,
    An' the bone poked right outer this limb.

' Fer a spell I felt horribly sick
    While I held there a meetin' of *me ;*
Proposed—' It is U P with Dick,'
    Put, an' carried unanermously.
Broken-legged, fifteen mile from the Creek—
    I weighed chances, an' gave up the case,
But I didn't deal fair by The Freak,
Till he limped to me, staggered an' weak,
    An' he flopped his ole lip in my face.

' Do? I fondled his nose like a fool,
    An' I called him love names without end ;
Though I ain't a soft man as a rule,
    There is times when I sorter unbend.
'Taint no use now to talk of the pain,
    I endoored ez I struggled to climb
To his back from a log, or explain
How I fell back again an' again ;
    But I gave up exhausted in time,

' An' I flung myself down on the ground,
   An' I cursed an', yes, maybe I cried,
But The Freak he came nosin' around,
   An' he rolled over right by my side.
Don't *you* try to explain, I'm content
   That he *knew* jest ez well ez could be,
'Cos I looked in his eyes ez he bent,
By the Lord, an' I *saw* what he meant,
   An' that's good enough talkin' fer me.

' Well, I crawled on his back ez he lay,
   An' he heaved himself up again, so,
An' then struck out fer home, an' till day
   I hung on to him, how I don't know.
Not a thing do I mind after that
   'Fore I came round all right at the whim,
Spread out on the bunk of Big Mat,
With a doc. on the job from The Flat,
   An' my leg fairly timbered and trim.

' Yes, I've heard all the mag of the men—
   That he wanted to roll or to die,
An' it's true that he's kicked me since then,
   An' he's likewise uncommonly sly ;

But *I'm here.*   If they talk fer a week
    That one fact isn't goin' to change,
An' I owe it this day to The Freak
That a crow isn't clippin' his beak
    On my rib-bones out back by the range.'

IN TOWN

Out of work and out of money—out of friends that
    means, you bet—
Out of firewood, togs and tucker, out of everything
    but debt—
And I loathe the barren pavements, and the crowds
    a fellow meets,
And the maddening repetition of the suffocating
    streets.

With their stinks my soul is tainted, and the tang is
    on my tongue
Of that sour and smoky suburb and the push we're
    thrown among,
And I sicken at the corners polished free of paint
    and mirk
By the shoulders of the men who're always hanging
    round for work.

Home—good Lord! a three-roomed hovel 'twixt a
      puddle and a drain,
In harmonious connection on the left with Liver
      Lane,
Where a crippled man is dying, and a horde of
      children fight,
And a woman in the horrors howls remorsefully at
      night.

It has stables close behind it, and an ash-heap for
      a lawn,
And is furnished with the tickets of the things we
      have in pawn ;
And all day the place is haunted by a melancholy
      crowd
Who beg everything or borrow, and to steal are not
      too proud.

Through the day come weary women, too, with
      famine-haunted eyes,
Hawking things that are not wanted—things that no
      one ever buys.
And I hate the prying neighbours, in their animal
      content,
And the devilish persistence of the man who wants
      the rent.

I, who cared for none, and faltered at no work a
 man might do,
Felt a fierce delight possess me when the trucks
 went surging through,
When the flood raced in the sluices, or the giant
 gums swung round
'Fore my axe, and flung their mighty limbs all
 mangled on the ground—

I who hewed and built and burrowed, and who asked
 no man to give
When a strong arm was excuse enough for venturing
 to live—
I am creeping by the gutters, with a simper and a
 smirk,
To the Fates in spats and toppers for the privilege
 of *work*.

Far away the hills are all aflame ; the blossom golden
 fair
Streams up the gladdened ranges, and its scent is
 everywhere,
And the kiddies of the settlers on the creek are
 red and sweet,
Whilst my youngsters have the sallowness and
 savour of the street.

To escape these endless vaults of brick, and pitch a
     tent out back,
If I get a chance I'll graft until my very sinews
     crack.
Meanwhile may all the angels up in Paradise look
     down
On a man of sin who died not, but was damned and
     sent to town.

THE DESERTED HOMESTEAD

Past a dull, grey plain where a world-old grief seems
    to brood o'er the silent land,
When the orbéd moon turns her tense, white face on
    the ominous waste of sand,
And the wind that steals by the dreamer feels like
    the touch of a phantom hand,

Through the tall, still trees and the tangled scrub
    that has sprung on the old bush track,
In a clearing wide, where a willow broods and the
    cowering bush shrinks back,
Stands a house alone that no dwellers own, yet un-
    harmed by the storm's attack.

137

'Tis a strange, sad place. On the shingle roof
    mosses gather and corn-blades spring,
And a stillness reigns in the air unstirred by the
    beat of a wild bird's wing.
He who sees believes that the old house grieves
    with the grief of a sentient thing.

From the charméd gums that about the land in a
    reverent circle throng
Comes no parrot's call, nor the wild-cat's cry, nor
    the magpie's mellow song,
And their shadows chill with an icy thrill and the
    sense of an awful wrong.

And the creek winds by 'neath the twisted briar and
    the curling creepers here ;
In the dusky depths of its bed it slips on its slime-
    green rocks in fear,
And it murmurs low to its stealthy flow in a monotone
    quaint and drear.

On a furrowed paddock that fronts the house grow
    the saplings straight and tall,
And noxious weeds in the garden ground on the
    desolate pathways crawl ;
But the briar twists back with the supple-jack 'tween
    the rocks of the rubble wall.

On the rotting walls of the gloomy rooms bats gather
    with elfin wings,
And a snake is coiled by the shattered door where a
    giant lizard clings,
For this house of care is the fitting lair of a myriad
    voiceless things.

Once I camped alone on the clearing's edge through
    the lapse of a livelong night,
When the wan moon flooded the house and land in a
    lake of her ghostly light,
And the silence dread of a world long dead filled my
    credulous soul with fright.

For no wind breathed by, but a nameless awe was
    abroad in the open there,
And the camp fire burned with a pale, thin flame in
    the chill, translucent air,
And my dog lay prone, like a chiselled stone, with
    his opaline eyes a-stare.

In the trancéd air was an omen felt and the sway of
    a subtle spell,
And I waited long for I knew not what, but the
    pale night augured well—
At a doleful hour, when the dead have power, lo! a
    hideous thing befell.

From the shadows flung by the far bush wall
    came a treacherous, phantom crew,
Like the smoke rack blown o'er the plain at morn
    when the bracken is wet with dew.
Not a sound they made, and their forms no shade on
    the moonlit surface threw.

And the night was changed to the quiet eve of a
    beautiful summer's day,
And the old house warmed as with life and light, and
    was set in a garden gay,
And a babe that crawled by the doorway called to a
    kitten that leapt in play.

But the black fiends circled the peaceful home, and I
    fathomed their evil quest ;
From the ground up-springing they hurled their
    spears, and danced with a demon zest,
And a girl lay dead 'neath the roses red with a
    wound in her fair, white breast.

Through the loopéd wall spat a rifle's flame, and the
    devilish pack gave tongue,
For a lean form writhed in a torment dire, on the
    crimsoned stubble flung.
Many echoes spoke, and the sluggish smoke on the
    shingles rolled and clung.

Yet again and oft did the flame spring forth, and
    each shaft from the dwelling shore
Through a savage heart, but the band unawed at
    the walls of the homestead tore,
And a man and wife fought for love and life with
    the horde by the broken door.

Then ghostly and grey, from the dusky bush came
    a company riding fast.
Seven horses strode on the buoyant air, and I
    trembled and gazed aghast,
Such a deadly hate on the forehead sate of each rider
    racing past.

With a cry they leapt on the dusky crew, and swept
    them aside like corn
In the lusty stroke of the mower's scythe, and
    distracted and overborne
Many demons fled, and left many dead, by the hoofs
    of the horses torn.

Not in vain—not all—though a father lay with the
    light on his cold, grey face,
And a mother bled, with a murdered maid held
    close in a last embrace,
For the babe laughed back at a visage black death
    drawn to a foul grimace.

Came a soft wind swaying the pendent leaves, like
    the sigh of awakening day,
And the darkness fell on my tired eyes, for the
    phantoms had passed away;
And the breezes bore from a distant shore faint
    echoes of ocean's play.

Past a dull, grey plain, through the tall, still trees,
    where the lingering days inspire
An unspoken woe in the heart of man, and the nights
    hold visions dire,
Stands a house alone that no dwellers own, yet
    unmarred by the storm or fire.

A NEW GIRL UP AT WHITE'S

There's a fresh track down the paddock
    Through the lightwoods to the creek,
And I notice Billy Craddock
    And Maloney do not speak,
And The Snag is slyly bitter
    When he's criticising Bill,
And there's quite a foreign glitter
    On the fellows at the mill.

Sid M'Mahon's turned out a dandy
    With a masher coat and tie,
And the engine-driver, Sandy,
    Curls his whiskers on the sly:
All the boys wear paper collars
    And their tombstone shirts of nights,
So it's ten to one in dollars
    There's a new girl up at White's.

She's a charmer from the river,
    But she steeps the lads in gloom,
With her blue eyes all a-quiver
    And her hair like wattle-bloom;
Though she's pretty and beguiling,
    And so lit up, like, with fun
That the flowers turn to her smiling,
    Just as if she was the sun.

But I wish she'd leave the valley,
    For the camp is dull to me,
Now the mill hands never rally
    For the regulation spree,
And there's not another joker
    Gives a tinker's curse for nap.,
Or will take a hand at poker
    Or at euchre with a chap!

Tom won't stir us with his fiddle
    By the boilers as he did
While Bob stepped it in the middle,
    And we passed the billy-lid.
Ah! we had some gay old nights there,
    But the boys now don't agree,
And they hang about at White's there,
    When they've togged up after tea.

With the gloves we have no battle;
  Now they sneak away and moon
Round with White, discussing cattle
  All the Sunday afternoon.
There's a want of old uprightness,
  Too, has come upon the push,
And a sort of cold politeness
  That's not called for in the bush.

They're all off, too, in that quarter;
  Kate goes sev'ral times a week
Seeing Andy Kelly's daughter,
  Jimmy's sister, up the creek;
And this difference seems a pity,
  Since their chances are so slim—
While they're running after Kitty,
  She is running after Jim.

' Harry ! what, that yourself, back to old Vic., man,
Down from the Never Land ?   Now, what's your
      game ?
Ugly as ever.   Not dropped the old trick, man ?
Say, what'll you take with me ?   Give it a name.

' Here long ?   Well, rather, lad ; five years and over,
Settled for good, and supporting a wife.
Slipped from the saddle, and living in clover,
Swore off a heap, and I've slung the old life.

' What's come of Taffy, and Brum, and the rest of
      them ?
Long since you broke with the Poverty push ? '
' Bill, you're on top, you've the best of the best of
      them.
Poor Brum's a dummy, Taff died in the bush ;

' Bob's cook for Chows on an absentee's station,
Sam's tout for spielers, Pete's lumbered for life ;
I'm on a tramp through the whole of creation,
Tracking a woman, my runaway wife.

' Left me six years ago—sloped !   I was shearing
Up on the Thomson.   She left not a word ;
Last year was seen by a Barcoo man, steering
Round about here, and that's all that I've heard.

' Heard of her, know her, Bill ?—tallish and clever,
Blue eyes, dark hair, and she's branded here, so ;
Not one to liquor, or go on the never,
But skittish and queer, in her tantrums, you know.

' This is her picture, Bill ; just have a look at her.
Like any female you chance to have seen ?
Hallo ! here, hold up ! Say, man, what's the matter?
YOUR WIFE !   By the Lord, Morton, what do you
        mean ? '

He was working on a station in the Western when I
    knew him,
And he came from Conongamo, up the old sur-
    veyors' track,
And the fellows all admitted that no man in Vic.
    could 'do him,'
Since he'd smothered Stonewall Menzie, also Ander-
    son, the black.
Bob was modelled for a fighter, but he'd run to
    beef a trifle;
For his science every rouseabout was satisfied to
    vouch,
And Red Fogarty advised us he delivered like a rifle,
And his stopping—well, beside him Harry Sallars
    was a slouch.

Not a man of us had met him till he settled on
    the station—
This was early in the Sixties, what we call the
    good old days—

And it's cheerfully admitted Robert owed his
    reputation
To a crippled jaw, a broken nose, and eyes that
    looked both ways.
We were certain on the face of it our guess was not
    an error,
Every feature of his phiz was marked, his chin was
    pulled askew,
And The Critic passed the office : ' Bet your buttons
    he's a terror !
That's the man who hammered Kelly on The Creek
    in Fifty-two ! '

Bob was not a shrinking blossom, and he helped the
    first impressions
By his subsequent admissions to the ringers and
    the mugs,
And he let himself be tickled into casual confessions
Of his battles with the bruisers and the scientific
    pugs.
How he'd mangled Matty Hardy was his earliest
    narration ;
He'd completely flummoxed Kitchen, and had made
    the climate hot
For Maloney, Fee, and Curran. It was quite a
    consolation
When he graciously informed us that he hadn't
    licked the lot.

The arrival of the Wonder gave a spurt to local
    science,
And we had an exhibition every evening in the
    week,
For the lightest joke was answered in the lingo of
    defiance,
And our blood was cast like water on the grasses by
    the creek.
Every fellow but the stranger had his scrap or
    rough-and-tumble ;
No one thought of looking ugly at the slugger,
    Battered Bob ;
And whene'er the boys addressed him 'twas in
    language choice and humble,—
Though they ached to see him beaten, none was
    anxious for the job.

How we honoured Bob, and yielded to his later
    information ;
Let him lead in all the arguments, and gently run
    the ranche !
And a very small potato was the owner of the
    station
By the man who slaughtered Melody and fought a
    draw with Blanche.
Battered Bob became our champion, our boss, and
    by degrees he

Sent his fame down to the Wannon, and right up
    to Spooner's Gap,
And he scooped the honours smiling, and he held
    them just as easy,
For we'd never seen him shape yet, and he hadn't
    fought a tap.

We'd a cook whose name was Han Cat—he was
    short, and fat, and yellow,
Just a common, ugly Chinky, with a never ending
    smile.
Bob was careful to avoid the corns of any other
    fellow,
But he filled Han Cat with sorrow, and he whaled
    him all the while.
Han Cat groaned and bore it meekly, and we didn't
    care to figure
In the antics of the Champion or his little private
    rows.
Robert said, 'I like a native, and I'll liquor with a
    nigger,
But I hate the skin and colour of these sanguinary
    Chows!'

On a certain Sunday morning Robert slyly cut a
    section
Off the pig-tail of the pagan—'twas Han's glory
    and his pride—

But the trouble that came after is his saddest
    recollection,
And the boys were so disgusted that they very
    nearly died.
Han Cat wept a while, and then he turned and
    scowled as black as thunder,
And he cursed the grinning spoiler till he had to
    stop for breath :
When he shaped up like a Christian, and he waltzed
    into the Wonder,
We arranged a ring, and waited for the heathen's
    sudden death.

Oh! the sorrow of that Sunday! Oh! the shame
    and degradation!
The chaps were simply paralyzed, and everyone was
    dumb,
For the heathen pushed the battle in the fashion of
    our nation,
And he countered in a way that made the Wonder
    fairly hum.
' Bob is fooling Han,' we murmured, ' he'll surprise
    him in a minute—
Soon he'll rise to this occasion, and display his
    proper form ! '
But, alas! we'd nursed a viper, for our pug was
    never in it—

And he couldn't battle well enough to keep the
Pagan warm.

Han Cat beat our battered champion, beat the
conqueror of Menzie,
And he towed him round the paddock like a dummy
stuffed with hair,
And we never stirred to interfere and stop the
Chinky's frenzy
When he jumped upon the Wonder in a manner
most unfair.
You must fancy all our sorrow, and our shame and
indignation,
For pen can never, never tell how horrified we
felt.
In the morning Little Finney, for the credit of the
station,
Hammered Han in stylish fashion with one fist
tucked in his belt.

As for Robert, we discussed him in a serious con-
vention,
And resolved that we were victims of a duffer's
awful skite,
And we put it up to tar him ; but he dropped to our
intention,

And he skipped, without a character, for Hamilton
    that night.

There's a moral, boys: Don't think a mangled boko
    is a token

That a fellow is a fighter, as a simple thing of
    course;

Like Battered Bob, he may have had his features
    bent and broken

Through his carelessness when drunk in being
    walked on by a horse.

THE SPLITTER

In the morn when the keen blade bites the tree,
 And the chips on the dead leaves dance,
And the bush echoes back right merrily
 Blow for blow as the sunbeams glance
From the axe when it sweeps in circles true,
 Then the splitter at heart is gay ;
He exults in the work he's set to do,
 And he feels like a boy at play.

Swinging free with a stroke that's straight and strong
 To the heart of the messmate sent,
He is cheered by the magpie's morning song
 With the ring of the metal blent,
But the birds in their terror scatter high
 When she falls with a rush and bound,
And the quivering saplings split and fly,
 And the ranges all roar around.

Who is lord when the axeman mounts his spar,
　　And the breeze on his brown breast blows,
When the scent of the new wood floats afar,
　　And the gum from its red wounds flows ?
With the bush at his back he laughs at care,
　　With a pipe and a right good mate—
There is drink in the billy, grub to spare,
　　And a bunk in the ten-by-eight.

When the sun's in the west, from nooks aloft
　　Where the stringy is straight and tall,
Come the strains of a chorus quaint and soft,
　　Or the clink of the wedge and maul ;
From the gully a murmur of broken talk
　　Or the song that the crosscut sings ;
For the bush is a-dream, and high the hawk
　　Hangs at rest on his cradling wings.

But at night, by the tent, when tea is done
　　And when euchre's begun to flag—
In the bush he may hear a distant gun
　　Or the neigh of a lonely nag—
Then the splitter has thoughts no longer gay,
　　And sorrows he cannot drown,
For he dreams of a girl who's far away,
　　Or the joys of a spree in town.

TO THE THEORETICAL SELECTOR

Would you be the King, the strong man, first in
    council and in toil,
To the men who war with nature for possession of
    the soil?
Take an axe upon your shoulder, take a billy and a
    rug,
And go forward in the forest where no man has cut
    and dug,
Where the scrub-ferns grow like magic, and the
    gum-trees you must fell
Have their topmost boughs in heaven, and their
    tap-roots deep as hell.

Take the land the Powers would cheerfully devote
    to Smith or Brown,
Two miles or more from water and a hundred miles
    from town ;

Fell, and scrub, and hew, and hunger, and when
    seven weeks are gone
You may have a clearing large enough to build a hut
    upon.
Then you furnish it with saplings and you carpet it
    with loam,
And you bring the kids and missus to their charming
    country home !

Rising early with the jackass, like a man of pith
    and push,
With axe in hand you sally forth to face the stubborn
    bush.
'Tis a mighty undertaking, and the odds are hard
    enough,
But the settler must be stubborn, and the settler
    must be tough,
And he strikes from morn till even with his strong
    arm bare and brown,
And he counts his gains by inches when the big gum
    rattles down.

So you slave and strive and suffer, for it's fearful
    work and slow
Ere the cabbages are solid and the spuds have room
    to grow.

By and bye to fruit and fowls and swine, as city
    swells advise,
You resort to make a fortune; but the venture
    proves unwise,
For the fruit-trees blight and wither, and the pigs
    die in their pens,
And the drought destroys the ducklings, and the
    dingoes eat the hens.

Years go on, and still the bush-wall rings your narrow
    clearing round,
But you've won a few good acres and a crop is on
    the ground,
And you harvest single-handed and you rake the
    stubble clean,
For you lack the cash for wages and the marvellous
    machine:
Still you're thankful for small mercies—though
    you're often sorely pushed—
When the missus hasn't sunstroke and the baby
    isn't bushed.

Then, at last, when worn with work, and warped with
    years, and very grey,
When you're mastering the mortgage and the rail-
    road runs your way,

When your farm is looking home-like, and your sons
    are grown-up men,
You may talk to brown-faced farmers—you may try
    to teach them then.
And if any kid-gloved critic starts to give you
    points on grain,
And a little hot-house farming does to make your
    errors plain,
You will rise up with a waddy, and you'll sympathise
    with Cain.

BULLOCKY BILL

From a river siding, the railway town,
Or the dull new port there three days down,
Forward and back on the up-hill track,
With a creak of the jinker, a ringing crack,
Slow as a funeral, sure as steam,
Bullocky Bill and his old red team.

Ploughing around by the ti-tree scrub,
Four wheels down to the creeping hub,
Swaying they go, with their heads all low,
Bally, and Splodger, and Spot, and Jo.
Men in the ranges much esteem
Bullocky Bill and his old red team.

Worming about where the tall trees spring,
Surging ahead when the clay bogs cling;

A rattle of lash and of language rash
On the narrow edge of immortal smash.
He'd thread a bead or walk a beam,
Bullocky Bill with his old red team.

Climbing a ridge where the red stars ride ;
Straddling down on the other side,
With a whistle and grind, and a scramble blind,
And a thundering gum-tree slung behind.
But they always get there, hill or stream,
Bullocky Bill and his old red team.

Engines or stamps for the mines abont,
Tools for the men who are leading out ;
Tucker, and boose, and the latest news
Back where the bunyip stirs the ooze.
Pioneers with the best we deem
Bullocky Bill and his old red team.

THE DROVERS IN REPLY

We are wondering why those fellows who are writing
    cheerful ditties
Of the rosy times out droving, and the dust and
    death of cities,
Do not leave the dreary office, ask a drover for a
    billet,
And enjoy 'the views,' 'the campfires,' and 'the
    freedom' while they fill it.

If it's fun to travel cattle or to picnic with merinoes,
Well the drover doesn't see it—few poetic raptures
    he knows.
As for sleeping on the plains beneath 'the pale
    moon' always seen there,
That is most appreciated by the man who's never
    been there.

And the ' balmy air,' the horses, and the ' wondrous
    constellations,'
The 'possum-rugs, and billies, and the tough and
    musty rations,
It's strange they only please the swell in urban
    streets residing,
Where the trams are always handy if he has a taste
    for riding.

We have travelled far with cattle for the very best
    of reasons—
For a living—we've gone droving in all latitudes and
    seasons,
But have never had a mate content with pleasures of
    this kidney,
And who wouldn't change his blisses for a flutter
    down in Sydney.

Night-watches are delightful when the stars are
    really splendid
To the sentimental stranger, but his joy is quickly
    ended
When the rain comes down in sluice-heads, or the
    cutting hailstones pelter,
And the sheep drift with the blizzard, and the horses
    bolt for shelter.

Don't imagine we are soured, but it's peculiarly
    annoying
To be told by city writers of the pleasures we're
    enjoying,
When perhaps we've nothing better than some fluky
    water handy,
Whilst the scribes in showy bar-rooms take iced
    seltzer with their brandy.

The dust in town is nothing to the dust the drover
    curses,
And the dust a drover swallows, and the awful thirst
    he nurses
When he's on the hard macadam, where the wethers
    cannot browse, and
The sirocco drives right at him, and he follows twenty
    thousand.

This droving on the plain is really charming when
    the weather
Isn't hot enough to curl the soles right off your
    upper leather,
Or so cold that when the morning wind comes hissing
    through the grasses
You can feel it cut your eyelids like a whip-lash as
    it passes.

There are bull-ants in the blankets, wicked horses,
    cramps, and ' skeeters,'
And a drinking boss like Halligan, or one like
    Humpy Peters,
Who is mean about the rations, and a flowing stream
    of curses
From the break of day to camping, through good
    fortune and reverses.

Yes, we wonder why the fellows who are building
    chipper ditties
Of the rosy times out droving and the dust and
    death of cities,
Do not quit the stuffy office, ask old Peters for a
    billet,
And enjoy the stars, the camp-fires, and the freedom
    while they fill it.

THE SHANTY

There are tracks through the scrub, there's a track
     down the hill,
And a track round the bend from M'Courteney's
     mill,
Where they slyly emerge from the bush and con-
     verge,
You'll discover the humpy—the theme of this
     dirge—
That is used for the sale of O'Sullivan's ' purge.'
     And if curses and cries,
     And a blasting of eyes,
   And a series of blasphemies fearful arise,
     And a lunatic din,
     And a racket like sin,
   You can bet all you own the O'Sullivan's in.

It's a bark and slab hut, with a bar and a bunk,
And a man propped before it disgustingly drunk,
And a nameless galoot in a hand-me-down suit,
Straddling out on the grass, grim as death, and as
      mute,
Trapping millions of rabbits that run from his boot.
      When eleven lie round
      In all shapes on the mound,
   And two navvies are fighting like fiends on the
      ground,
      'Tisn't needful to say
      It's the sweet Sabbath day,
   And that trade at the shanty's uncommonly gay.

Mrs. O'. makes the drinks, and O'Sullivan's dart
Is to drink all he can to keep others in heart.
Though he's old in the hoof, and he reckons he's
      proof
'Gainst infernalest liquors, in warp and in woof,
He's quite frequently seen howling out on the roof.
      For from fungus or fruits,
      From old rags or from roots,
   Grass, cabbages, pickles, old bedding or boots,
      Or the leaves of the gum,
      Or whatever may come,
   Mrs. O'. can extract the most 'illigant' rum.

They've no peace in the hut and no peace on the hill,
Mrs. O'. never sleeps and her hand's never still;
And old constable Mack cannot hit on the track
As a man of the law.   As a stranger in black
When he finds his way there he can't find his way back.
  There's no signboard to see,
  But those fools on the spree,
 Or a man in his shirt shrieking prayers to a tree.
  As for licenses—yar!
  They don't know what they are,
For they drink without license at Sullivan's bar.

AH LING, THE LEPER

Up a dark and fetid alley, where the offal and the
    slime
Of a brave and blusterous city met its misery and
    crime,
In a hovel reeking pestilence, and noisome as the
    grave,
Dwelt Ah Ling, the Chinese joiner, and the sweater's
    willing slave.

Squatting down amongst the shavings, with his chisel
    and his plane,
Through the long, hot days of striving, dead to
    pleasure and to pain,
Like a creature barely human, very yellow, gaunt,
    and grim,
Ah Ling laboured on, for pleasure spread no lures
    that tempted him.

170

And the curious people, watching through the rotten
    wall at night,
Saw his death's face weirdly outlined in the candle's
    feeble light ;
Saw him still intent upon his work, ill-omened and
    unclean,
Planing, sawing, nailing, hewing—just a skin and
    bone machine.

Neither kith nor kin the joiner had; perchance he
    nerved his hand
With the treasured hope of seeing once again his
    native land
As a Chinaman of fortune, and of finishing his life
At his ease in China Proper, with a painted Chinese
    wife.

But Ah Ling grew yet more grisly, and 'twas easy
    now to trace
Signs of vice and fierce privations in his scarred and
    pitted face,
With a dreadful something added. By this thing
    the truth was known,
And his countrymen forsook him, and he lived and
    toiled alone.

Still the work came in, and still he slaved and saw
　　　his earnings grow.
Who's to trouble where the goods are made when
　　　buyers will not know?
Gimcrack chairs and pretty nick-nacks from infected
　　　dens like this
Go to furnish happy homes to-day where ignorance
　　　is bliss.

Now the time was come when Ling might take his
　　　treasure up, and go
To enjoy celestial comforts by the flowing Hoang Ho,
But one day his shop was raided, and upon him fell
　　　the hand
Of the Law—and death were better than the ruthless
　　　Law's command.

'Room for the leper, room!' A thing of fear, Ah
　　　Ling was torn
From his hovel and his labour and his cherished
　　　hopes, and borne
To a home of untold terrors, where to life grim
　　　death is wed,
And the quick behold and know the loathly horrors
　　　of the dead.

THE EMU OF WHROO

We've a tale to tell you of a spavined emu,
  A bird with a smile like a crack in a hat,
Who was owned by M'Cue, of the township of
    Whroo,
  The county of Rodney—his front name was Pat.
The bird was a dandy, although a bit bandy,
  Her knees, too, were queer and her neck out of
    gauge—
She'd eat what was handy, from crowbars to candy,
  Was tall, too, and tough for a chick of her age.
But her taste and her height, and her figure and
    smile,
Were the smallest potatoes compared with her guile.

M'Cue's bird had a name, Arabella that same—
  A name that was given by Pat, we may say,
To the memory and fame of a red-headed flame,

Because, as he said, ' she wuz builded that way.'
The bird Arabella let nothing compel her,
  Her temper was bad when disturbed, as a rule.
She'd rupture the smeller of any young ' feller '
  Who teased, with a kick that would honour a mule.
And the boys and the girls who were then living near
Were all minus an eye—those with luck had one ear.

The emu with her smile would the new-chum beguile
  To step up and study the great, gawky bird,
And then let out in style, and she'd hoist him a mile—
  The sound of his wailing would never be heard.
At which she'd look stately, and mild, and sedately,
  And seem to be steeped in some deep inward woe,
Or wondering greatly what happened there lately
  That people found need to go tearing round so.
P. M'Cue overlooked his long bird's little craze,
He declared it was only her emusing ways.

Is it strange that in time these outrages should prime
  The neighbours with ire and profanity dread ?
And at every crime, with good reason and rhyme,
  They'd bombard the bird with old iron and lead ;
Their weapons would whistle by Bella and hiss ill,
  The bird only smiled as they yearned for her gore ;

They wasted their gristle, she ate up each missile,
   And placidly looked on and waited for more.
Her digestion not stones nor old nails could upset,
So it's strange that the men disagreed with the pet.

The late Mr. M'Cue, of the township of Whroo,
   Would hear no complaints of his biped absurd,
And with little ado put the biggest man through
   Who'd lay ' e'er a finger' on Bella, the bird.
If father or teacher came flaunting a feature
   Removed from a boy, say, an eyelid or ear,
He sooled on the preacher his feathery creature,
   Or offered to fight him for money or beer.
And to shoot at this bird was but labour in vain,
She digested their slugs and she faced them again.

But M'Cue for his care and anxiety rare
   Got meagre rewards from his camel-shanked fowl.
For when on a tear she'd uproot his back hair
   And peck at his ear and snatch scraps off his jowl.
A kick from the shoulder, a shock like a boulder
   That weighed half-a-ton being twisted in quick,
And Patrick was older and very near cold ere
   The time he recovered that feathered mule's kick.
At the worst he but sighed, and regretfully said
It reminded him so of his wife who was dead.

But the time came at last when anxiety cast
   Its spell o'er the bird, she grew dull and deprest—
She felt glum, and she passed to hysterics as fast—
   All day she sought round in sore mental unrest.
She acted like moody, hysterical Judy,
   When Punch is inspired for a villainous lark;
But Paddy was shrewd—he could see she was broody
   And yearned in the chick-rearing biz to embark.
The momentous importance and stress of her case
Were quite plain in her actions and seen in her face.

She tried sitting on stones, and on brickbats, and bones,
   But moped all the time and supped grief to the
      dregs—
There was nothing in cones, and in harrowing tones
   She spoke her great yearning to cultivate eggs.
One morning, day-dreaming, all glossy and gleaming
   She saw the bald head of the neighbour next door;
Its round, egg-like seeming, set Bell wildly scheming
   To sit on that skull or be happy no more;
And she laid for the man by the dark and the day,
And he cursed and he kicked in a terrible way.

From that day, it is said, Arabella she led
   The bald-headed men who live near a hard life;

They all held her in dread—for her manners ill-bred
  M'Cue spent his time in tempestuous strife.
With eye speculative, she cornered each native
  To find if his skull would just suit her complaint;
The man's strength was great if he saved all his
    pate, if
  She failed to secure half his scalp in distraint.
And her owner indulged in Satanic delights,
And he egged on his bird to more furious fights.

But the downfall of spite and the triumph of right
  Are bound to come round, fight we ever so hard;
On one March morning bright, Old M'Cue very
    tight,
  Returned to his home and dossed down in the yard.
He'd not long been sleeping when Bella came
    peeping
  And viewed with delight his bare head, like a cast,
And into her keeping she raked it, and heaping
  Her ribs on the skull she was happy at last.
And she sat till the day and the night both were
    gone,
And the next day and next was she still sitting on.

It was thought Pat had fled, and a week or more sped
  E'er folks came to search, and they found for their
    pains

P. M'Cue lying dead with the bird on his head
　　Still stolidly striving to hatch out some brains.
No priest at Pat's croaking, by blessings invoking,
　　Had served to make easy the poor sinner's death.
Some folks blamed his soaking, the jury said
　　　　' choking '—
　　The bird was found guilty of stopping his breath,
And for peace, and for quiet, and morality's sake
She was killed with a slab from a Cousin Jack cake.